BROKEN PROMISES

An Anthology

BROKEN PROMISES

An Anthology

Presented by

The Dublin Creative Writers Cooperative

Dublin, Ohio

Published by
SPARKSTREET MEDIA LLC
HTTP://WWW.SPARKSTREETMEDIA.COM/

PO Box 3155
Dublin, Ohio 43016

BROKEN PROMISES: An Anthology

Presented by The Dublin Creative Writers Cooperative
Dublin, Ohio

Curated by J. Powell Ogden

Edited by Anita Howitt

Copyedited by Anne-Marie Neal
WWW.ANNEMARIENEAL.COM

Interior Design and Formatting by We Got You Covered Book Design
WWW.WEGOTYOUCOVEREDBOOKDESIGN.COM

Paperback ISBN: 978-0-9989551-7-9
Ebook ISBN: 978-0-9989551-8-6

Grateful acknowledgement is made for permission to include both print and digital copies of the following stories in this anthology. All authors listed below retain full rights to their work, including the right to publish and reproduce them in print, digital or in any other form.

Printed in the United States of America

10 9 8 7 6 5 4 3 2 1

TABLE OF CONTENTS

“Sooner or later, everyone sits down
to a banquet of consequences.”

Robert Louis Stevenson

THE DUBLIN CREATIVE WRITERS COOPERATIVE
of Dublin, Ohio

PRESENTS

Members of the Dublin Creative Writers Cooperative are committed to working together to improve their craft. Our group welcomes those who are driven to publish, as well as those who just want to write. However, we really thrive on our members who have that feverish need to tell stories, whether true, or conjured from the imagination. We are lucky to have the writer who wakes up before dawn to get their pages in and dedicates hours of time encouraging and critiquing their fellow members' work and the writer who finds time between work and home, who learns from every draft written and read. We draw inspiration from the indie publisher, who designs every aspect of their book with the greatest detail, the author with the infectious laugh who calls in from another continent and the tenacious soul who writes with children on his lap, hanging off his shoulders, and crawling under the desk. These are the writers who, in this bizarre, fraught pandemic era, still fight for the time and mindfulness needed to get words on the page.

This anthology was created to give members at all levels the opportunity to showcase their stories and diverse talents. You'll find writers who have never been published, those who have had pieces published in journals and magazines, and a few who have multiple books on the market. During the process of creating this anthology, we have dedicated hours to working together, reading and critiquing each other's work, and cheering each other on with the aim to get our best stories out there.

Contributors were given only the premise of "broken promises" to play with, but common and unexpected themes emerged: marriage and infidelity, death and morality, myths, and the perilous sea. In this collection you will find flash fiction, short stories, and a novelette, written in a wide range of genres from fantasy to suspense to historical fiction. You will encounter starlets, monsters, pirates, and ghosts.

We have enjoyed putting this collection together, and we are confident you will find our tales to be valuable time spent. It is our hope that you'll laugh, gasp, snicker, and reflect as you read *Broken Promises: An Anthology.*

Thank you for your support in reading our work.

AUTUMN SHAH

Content Manager

October 2020

WRECKERS

By A. Howitt

"DO YOU SEE ANTHING?"

"It's only a matter of time now." Dozier closed up his spyglass. Night was on its way. Despite the smell of alewives rotting on the sand, conditions were perfect. His men, a dozen in all, milled about, some already celebrating with a drink.

"Get them into the shadows at least, Farrin. We don't need to draw attention."

As clouds filled the sky, Dozier pulled his cloak closed. The storm was coming. It was going to be a good night.

Captain Goodman started each day with a prayer. He named every sailor's saint, every old sea god, every goddess of good fortune and fair weather he could recall. The men in his charge probably thought him quite mad, but in his long career, he'd weathered some terrible storms at sea. His heart stuttered with every rumble of thunder.

With the light on the high hills guiding the *Shining Star* in, he called to his helmsman, "Steady on through the rain. We'll be at port before the worst of it hits."

"Aye, Captain," the helmsman called.

"I promised every hand a pint at dock tonight, and I'll be damned if this storm makes a liar of me." Goodman scanned the darkness with a spyglass he'd kept in his coat for a decade. Weather was a sailing man's worst enemy. Weather, and pirates.

Gerald clung to the gunwale as the ship lurched.

Breaking timbers, roaring winds.

He stared wildly into the darkness as rain stung his face.

"It's the wreckers! They've set a false light," Captain Goodman shouted, as the ship ran aground. "They've led us to the rocks!"

In the confusion, men jumped overboard.

The ship was going down.

Gerald wasn't the strongest swimmer, but he doubted it mattered. In a rough sea, no man had much chance unless he'd been born with gills. Gerald followed his comrades and threw himself overboard, praying Captain Goodman's gods would carry him safely to the beach in their hands. Or home to his mother, at least.

Dozier sent his wreckers into action. "Get the boats to the water."

Three to a boat, they headed into the waves, knives and hooks in hand. Three remained behind to help Dozier on the beach. Scouring the dark sand, the wreckers waited. Patience like growing oaks.

The first of the sailors and goods began washing up, and time was short. His men hauled crates and barrels away from the water's edge. Dozier stepped over the bodies of dead sailors, barking commands. The scavengers would hear the sounds of the wreck and the screams of sailors. They'd come running to loot what was left. Jackals.

A moan, nearby. Dozier searched and paused. He hovered over a half-drowned captain.

"Damn them what sets false lights," the captain hissed. "I promised their mothers..."

Dozier knelt and stuck his dagger into the man's chest. He took a brass compass from the captain's pocket. "Haul away what you can lads, it's time to go."

UNMARKED PASSAGE

By J. Levesque

WE REACH RUSSEL BEACON before sunset. Any later, and we would never have found this marker. The chart says it has a light, but an empty socket crowns the buoy's mutilated skeleton. As we approach, gulls squawk and flap and circle us before settling again on the rusting structure.

"Right on the money!" David pats my thigh.

I can't move farther away from him in our tiny sailboat.

"No fat-ass yachtsman could beat us with all the loran and radar in the world," he says. "What a team we are."

Apparently not. He is an amazing navigator, though. On my own, I could never plot the course and keep to it.

David stands tall and stretches as he always does. Five hours at the helm ties knots in his muscles. When he smiles, the skin at the corners of his brown eyes folds like paper fans. But when he embraces me, I stiffen.

"Sue." He squeezes hard then pushes me away. "Don't do this."

I despise diminutives. Sue. Liz. *Your lover always, Liz.*

Use my full name, I should say. *Call me Suzanna.* Instead, I remain silent and hope he feels my hate. I refuse to weep. I will not think about the letter.

Northeast of the beacon, we anchor in twenty feet of water, above conchs and sea stars that stroll serenely below. Beyond lies a rift in the ocean, a mile deep, lightless, and cold.

We tie a stern line to the beacon, having learned a lesson the night before.

At the sound of a boat horn, we had awakened to realize we were drifting, our anchor dragged by insistent tides across a grassy bottom. Lights ashore on Cat Cay and atop nearby masts were our only reference points. Without them, we would have believed ourselves still firmly rooted in the island's lee. We steered toward them last night, tied off to the boat that warned us, and sat awake until dawn when they headed north and we continued on our southward journey. If we drift here, the only vessel at a dead beacon, we will have no point of reference and no guide. On the edge of the Northwest Channel, no land in sight means no landmarks.

"How about supper. Aren't you hungry?" David's cheeriness sounds forced.

"No, I'm not. But I'll see what there is." I dramatize my willingness to sacrifice for him.

How could he betray such love, such loyalty? He should be eaten up with guilt.

The dripping icebox holds three eggs, half a loaf of sweet Bimini bread, and the remnants of a snaky, needle-nosed reef fish we hooked near Gun Cay two days ago. I pull the fish out and smell it. Not pleasant. Probably not safe to eat. Just what he deserves.

I cut the last of the flesh from startling blue bones. The first time I served the razor- toothed creature, it was sweet and firm. A perfect meal, on a perfect voyage, on the perfect honeymoon, four months after our quiet wedding. Dinner over, I had tidied the cabin and stowed the few items that David had left in his seabag. There I found the letter.

I rip the last shreds of meat from spiny ribs, just as David ripped the paper into jagged bits after I showed it to him. After I read it again and again.

Now, I drop the naked bones into the garbage, tie the plastic sack shut, then toss it through the hatch to land on deck near the transom. It will reek before morning.

Tomatoes, peppers, and salt tears disguise the fish's uncertain flavor. I carry the finished meal topside and watch David devour it. Off the starboard beam, dark shapes surface and disappear into the water around us.

"Sharks," David says. "Hemingway wrote about them. The guidebook talks about it."

Masters of their element, they glide past us and circle the buoy. I watch them until the departing sun pulls shrouds over the rich green shallows of the Great Bahama Bank and the measureless blue Tongue of the Ocean.

Below deck, we lie in darkness. The sea doesn't lull us gently to sleep. It twists and tosses, like a bull shedding its rider. I struggle to stay on my half of the forward berth. After an hour, David mutters and slips into the main cabin to lower the centerboard. That fails to stabilize us. He struggles back to bed, and again we lie braced against the vessel's erratic motion. Currents hurl us against the bulkheads and each other. The gulls cry all night long.

Finally, I climb through the hatch over the berth and sit straddling the bow. A round, pewter moon shatters on the sea. Wind chills my right ear, coming from the east, across the deep, but I doubt its reality. It must be a ghost wind, for the water bears no evidence of its passing. Two wave trains march staccato from the northwest and the north. Neither leaves its mark upon the other. I sit on deck and stare at the slack anchor line, which rises and falls with the water's heartbeat.

"Tidal surge." David's voice is right behind me.

I don't respond.

"Listen, Sue, there's no sense in us going on to Chub Cay. I told you it was nothing with her. And besides, it's over. But if you can't enjoy this trip, we may as well turn back."

"No, I'm all right," I lie. "I'd rather go on as we planned."

That much is true. There is nothing good to go back to. It's all dead now. Perhaps ahead, something will change the past or bury it.

David wraps his arms around me and kisses my eyes. I turn away and cry, making no sound.

"You're not all right." His voice breaks. "I'm not all right. I can't take this. I can't live like this."

The letter said he's been living very well like this. My face is cold with wind and tears.

"I love you," he says. "I don't want to lose you. But at some point, I have to recognize my own needs. I have to survive. I have to take care of myself. If you can't put this behind you, we might as well split right now. I can't live with you hanging this guilt over my head."

I hate David for thinking of himself, but I reach out because I cannot let her have him.

We hold each other in the dark. The gulls complain and thrash their wings as we descend to bed. Soon we are both wet from living at sea and weeping and lovemaking.

David whispers devotion in my ear. He does not whisper apologies nor beg forgiveness. I lie quiet and remember the words of the letter, Liz's words. Dawn comes slowly.

"Let's get underway," David says, drawing me close, kissing my hair.

Outside the porthole, the sky awakens, pink and lavender. A calm sea welcomes us topside. David retrieves the stern line from the dead beacon, and I take my station at the bow. The wind has died, so he starts the engine.

"Okay, pull it in," he tells me.

I begin hauling the slack anchor line. As I do, I curl it carefully between my feet. Seventy- five feet, half the rode, lies in dripping ovals on the deck, but the boat still floats in place. The line tightens. It lies under the boat, extending toward the stern. We have drifted over the anchor. No matter how hard I pull, the line does not give.

"Don't you have it up yet?" David shouts.

"I can't free it. You try."

He uses his greater strength, but the line stays taut. He lies flat on the foredeck and grasps it just above the waterline.

"Shit." He sits up. "It's caught on the centerboard."

He pays out more line and whips it back and forth, trying to dislodge the loop that must have coiled around the extended stabilizer. Nothing happens.

"Try raising the centerboard," he says.

I lower myself through the forward hatch and make my way to the main cabin. When I try to turn the crank, it doesn't move. If we had a daggerboard instead of this hinged centerboard, I could easily pull it up, but with this arrangement, my efforts are useless. Pulling harder would only make the control cord fray and snap, leaving us with no stabilizer. This tiny sloop has no keel. Without the centerboard, we can't weather rough seas.

Returning to the bow, I tell him, "It's jammed."

He rummages in the aft locker for the rope ladder. "I guess I'll have to go over the side. Get my mask, would you?"

As I turn toward the hatch, his hand on my arm stops me.

"Wait." He points toward the base of the beacon, twenty yards away.

Fins break the surface, circle, and disappear. They do not belong to dolphins.

"Shit," he repeats.

"Why don't you sit a while," I say. "I'll fix breakfast."

Over French toast, he gazes at me with loving eyes. When he touches my cheek, I kiss his fingers and smile.

He strips to his swim trunks while I dump the table scraps into the garbage sack. Last night's fish carcass releases its sickening odor. I do not retie the bag.

"Keep watch," he says, scanning the waters. "Bang on the hull if you see fins."

He secures his mask and descends the ladder. I don't call his attention to the shapes off the port quarter. Once he dives beneath the hull, I empty the garbage overboard. Gulls scream.

Gray sharks rise and feed in the clouded sea. Though the dawn colors have left the sky, a red smear spreads across the ocean's surface.

CONSEQUENCES

By Thomas Brown

THERE WAS ONLY ONE seat left on the train, and the reason was obvious. But it was a forty-five-minute ride home, and my feet ached from a bad choice of shoes. Cute didn't necessarily make for comfort.

He was sitting in the window seat shivering, his sports coat wrapped tight across his chest. Outside it was nearly August and in the nineties, but he would be cold for a while. Repentance wasn't enough.

"Hi, is this seat taken?" I asked the shivering man.

He did his best to smile at me and brushed the seat off next to him, the dusting of snow falling to the floor. He said nothing, but his actions were enough. I sat down and felt the breeze right away.

I looked over his head at the black cloud, at the snow flurries falling on him. His hair was full of snowflakes, water dripping down his face as the snow melted. He leaned forward to shake the wintery mess from his head, but the cloud stayed in place, centered on him. It was his actions, after all, that had put it there.

I'm a journalist, so it's my nature to run to the fire, not away from it. Everyone on the train was curious about the cloud above his head, the cause for it, but I was the only one with the lack of tact to ask.

"So, which one did you break?"

He looked at me, hesitating. He was maybe thirty-five; he looked like a bank manager or something. He wore a decent suit, but it wasn't meant for snow. He took a deep breath and answered.

"Adultery. She had just gotten back from vacation with her family. It was the end of the day. I went into her office. It was just a kiss."

He sighed and looked at his lap.

"Just one. She was in tears the whole way I walked her to her train. Lucky she at least had a sweater with her." He brushed off some accumulation from his shoulder. "What am I going to say to my wife? It was just a fling, it was just a distraction, I don't love her, I…"

He broke down in tears, and I found myself giving a hug to an adulterer with a snow cloud following him. It wouldn't leave until he confessed to his wife.

Welcome to the new world, where consequences for poor choices were suddenly much more relevant.

Half an hour later, the man had composed himself and thanked me, getting off at his stop. He waved as he left, and I felt the temperature rise in my seat with him gone.

My stop arrived soon enough, and I walked to my car. A giant billboard, electronic with changing ads, showed me a sale on cherries and oranges, then it flipped to a message, not an ad. Sort of.

"You are not lost or alone, God has returned. Follow His Commandments and bask in the warmth of His love."

The font was definite; like a business card, sharp and direct. I thought of the card I handed out when asking questions, and it occurred to me that God had a better card than I did. No surprise there.

It had only been two weeks since the world had changed. Though many had adjusted, obviously, some people were still adapting to the new normal. I had turned in an article only earlier that day about a man and his wife who had spent years addicted to drugs. Their story was a living nightmare. They had prayed to be clean, to be saved, to just get some help. They woke up to find a social worker at their door with two beds available when there had been no help for years. The treatment took immediately, and their hunger for drugs and self-destruction was gone.

Was it God Himself, or the God effect? The God effect was the young man helping an old woman cross the street. It was stopping before going down the flight of steps at the park to help the woman with the stroller get to the bottom. It was offering the cab to the person running with a newspaper over her head while you wait for the next one with your umbrella.

God was what had happened to the man on the train. Pretty quickly someone guessed the correlation between the old Hebrew Ten Commandments and the lightning bolt striking down a gang banger who accidentally shot a kid in Chicago. Or a storm cloud above an adulterer.

I suddenly had more to write about than ever. The idea of violating the Commandments filled people with fear. Politicians became public servants, criminals rethought their lives, and free will seemed to recede.

That was what I was writing about. Not that it mattered, according to my editor. God did what God wanted. Punishment or praise, people got what was coming to them. But if they knew the consequence was the stick, then they didn't do those things. It didn't make people kind; it made them afraid of the consequences of their actions. They weren't sorry for doing something, they were sorry they got caught.

These were the thoughts I wrestled with, day in and day out, at work or riding home. There was no answer, it seemed.

I parked in front of my apartment and went to see the only consistent man in my life.

I opened the door and saw that hiding the toilet paper had not curbed his appetite. To the contrary, he had found the roll under the sink, somehow opened the door, and shredded the roll all over the floor. He jumped up on the arm of the couch and sat down. He cocked his black and white face to the side and let out a long questioning "Meeeeoooow?"

"Goddamnit, Mr. Mittens," I yelled.

I heard a rumble above me and looked up. A dark storm cloud formed above my head, and the first droplets of rain fell down, hitting my face. I growled and said nothing, knowing I would be spending part of my evening sitting in the bathtub, waiting for the cloud to go away.

Like I said, still getting used to consequences.

THE INTERVIEW
By J.H. Schiller

MOIRA SULLIVAN STARED INTO the mirror.

Her dead husband, Jack, stared back at her.

She tried to look through him at her reflection so she could wipe the tears of frustration and humiliation from her cheeks, but it was no use. As he had in life, Jack loomed large in any space he occupied. He watched her with a mocking smile.

Stupid, he whispered. *I tried to tell you, Mo. You're old and slow and stupid.*

She looked away, choking back a sob. He was right, of course—cruel as always, but right. The interview had proven that.

She'd been so hopeful, had wanted the job so badly. She *loved* the library. It had been her refuge for years, a place of quiet and order unlike the bitter hell of her home. When she'd seen the sign announcing open interviews, she'd hoped it was a message from God that her life was finally going to turn around. Wasn't she due a good turn? She'd cared for Jack as he smoked himself to death. She'd cooked for him, cleaned for him. Endured him.

And then near… near the end, she'd discovered that he'd spent every dime they had playing poker games on the computer, just one of the many reasons she hated the cursed things. She'd been clueless, as usual, because he'd always insisted on handling their money, right up to the end. *You've got no head for numbers, Mo.*

So here she was, 75 years old and crying like a baby in the bathroom of the public library. Her cheeks burned as the interview flashed through her mind once more. Oh, how that smarmy man had smirked at her when she'd handed him her résumé. *Did you* type *this?* he'd asked, incredulous. *On an actual typewriter?*

She should've given up then, but she'd smiled brightly and nattered on about being old-fashioned. She'd agonized over that résumé, trying to come up with clever ways to describe her years as a homemaker. She knew she had a way with words, and she'd been proud of what she'd produced.

In the end, it didn't matter.

The interview began with a timed alphanumeric sorting exercise. Moira was good with puzzles and patterns. She knew the correct answers to the sorting exercise as soon as it displayed on the computer screen, but she couldn't find the mouse to move the words and numbers around. She wanted to look at what the other candidates were doing, but that felt like cheating, so she raised her hand and asked for help. Her face burned with shame as the proctor loudly explained that the computer had a touch screen. By the time she got started, the timer was running out and it was time to start the next phase—a computer skills test. After Moira's third hesitant request for assistance, the hiring manager himself had stopped by her station and gently suggested that she "pursue a position better matched to her strengths."

Fresh tears flooded her eyes and her breath caught with a hitch.

Stop your sniveling, Jack sneered. *You're pathetic.*

Pathetic. It was Jack's favorite term for her, one he'd probably used more times than he'd said her name. As an expert on being pathetic, Moira knew the word had two primary definitions. The first was "pitiable," and she supposed that, at the moment—an elderly widow crying alone in a bathroom—she certainly fit the bill. The second was "contemptibly inadequate." As she looked at Jack's twisted face in the mirror, something in her shifted and she truly saw him for the first time in their 51 years together. She saw that *he* was the one who was contemptible. *He* was inadequate.

A surge of righteous anger boiled up in her chest.

"Shut the fuck up!" she screamed. She pulled back in shock, covering her mouth with one shaking hand. It was the first curse word she'd said out loud since the S-word at the age of twelve. Her mother had washed her mouth out with soap.

It felt good.

Really good.

So she said it again, even louder.

"Shut the *fuck* up!"

Jack recoiled. Moira gripped the straps of her purse and swung it at the mirror as hard as she could. The metal buckle smashed into Jack's nose with a sharp crack, creating a spiderweb of shattered glass. With that blow, she was answering every slight, every insult, every slap and pinch and shove. The force behind it came from somewhere deep inside her; somewhere filled not with hurt, but rage. She rode a wave of exultation not unlike the brief joy she'd felt on that day last year, the day she'd thought she was free of him at last. She'd been wrong then, but maybe now... maybe...

She heard a chorus of howling shrieks and looked up to find a thousand Jacks screaming in the shards of the broken mirror. He would never leave her alone. Never. Seven years of bad luck, she thought, as a bubble of helpless laughter burst free from her clenched lips. Her bad luck had begun the day she met Jack, and apparently it outlived even him. The feeling of triumph faded, and Moira began to sob in earnest. It would never end.

A young mother opened the bathroom door, pulling with her one of those ridiculous bulky strollers parents favored these days. The shrieks of an outraged baby and the whining questions of a grumpy toddler echoed from the tile walls. As always, Moira's heart ached when she saw mothers with their children—the pain of a hope never fulfilled. She ducked into the first stall as the mother wrestled the plastic contraption around the tight corner. If she had to be subjected to the pity of a stranger right now, she might actually die of shame.

Moira fished a cloth handkerchief from her purse and mopped her face. Behind her the toilet flushed—one of those automatic things that always scared the bejesus out of her. The flush was so violent that drops of water sprayed up from the toilet, spattering her skirt. She shivered with revulsion and inched away from the toilet. The door to the large stall next to her, which served both the handicapped and the diaper set, opened and closed with a click. The baby's cries quieted to irritable whimpers.

"Hello?"

The woman was *talking* to her? In the bathroom? Moira was glad she was not actually using the facilities. The thought of talking while… well, it would be quite awkward.

"Yes?" she said.

"Hi, John," the woman said. "Yes, we're still at the library. We had to leave story time because Isabelle started throwing a fit."

Ah. One of those wireless headset phone things.

Behind Moira, the toilet flushed again. She fled the bathroom.

By the time she reached the lobby, her legs were quivering. Moira knew she couldn't make the walk to the bus stop in this condition. She needed to sit down and collect herself. The confidence she'd felt as she prepared for the interview, the slim thread of hope she'd been clinging to, was gone. She couldn't take this anymore.

Maybe it was time to do what she'd considered doing for years, long before Jack was gone. Growing up a devout Catholic before the reforms of Vatican II, she'd been taught that suicide was a mortal sin. That wasn't what had stopped her, though—not really. She was no stranger to mortal sin. No, what stayed her hand was a still, small voice in the quiet of her soul that said, *Don't give up*. But what if that voice fell silent? Would she do it? Would she double down on her seat in Hell?

She pictured Jack's twisted face, shrieking at her from the mirror. She was already in hell.

Moira closed her eyes and took a seat on the bench below the community bulletin board, taking deep, steadying breaths. There was a bit of commotion on the other side of the library, coming from the direction of the bathroom. The aftereffects of her outburst must have been discovered. She smiled to herself. No one would think the sweet old lady sitting calmly on the bench was the cause of the wreckage. She felt slightly guilty about the extra work for the library staff and the expense to the city, but if she was considering going out with one last mortal sin, she may as well pile on the misdeeds.

Moira stood, sighing deeply, and turned to go. Her bag snagged on a thumbtack from the bulletin board and tugged a small sheet of newsprint free, causing it to flutter to the floor. It was about the size of the old PennySaver she remembered getting decades ago. The headline at the top of the page read "Odd Jobs & Specialized Services." She didn't think companies used newspapers for Help Wanted ads these days. It all seemed to be on the computer, like everything else. Now that she could see it better, the paper did look old and faded. Most of the print was smudged and virtually illegible, except for one large paragraph in the center column.

Seeking switchboard operator for high call volume environment. The successful candidate will have excellent judgment, discernment, and discretion in routing incoming calls for ultimate resolution. Experience using cord PBX switchboards a must. Don't miss this once in a lifetime opportunity! Call OL 9-6782 to schedule an interview.

Underneath was a small, grainy photo of a row of smiling young women wearing headsets, seated in front of an old-fashioned cordboard. The woman closest to the photographer was inserting a phone plug into a jack on the board.

Moira's eyes filled with tears.

Her first and only job, fresh out of high school, was as a switchboard operator for a private branch exchange at a long-defunct insurance company in the early 1960s. Looking back, her six years there were the happiest of her life. For the first—and, though she didn't know it at the time, only—time in her life, she'd had close girlfriends. Donna, Mary Catherine, and Pam worked with her for most of her time there. They'd eaten lunch together, talked about the men in their lives, laughed, occasionally cried...

But that all ended when she married Jack. He didn't think it was appropriate for a married woman to work. She'd been sad to leave the job, but she hadn't minded too much. Jack promised her they'd start a family right away, and being a mother was her one true ambition. And Jack.... She didn't want to think about it now.

Moira's heart was pounding. Could this be a sign? Perhaps all was not yet lost. She squinted at the paper again. The phone number was old, at least fifty years out of date. It used the 2L+4N format from the 50s and 60s. There was no way it would work with modern phones... was there?

Only one way to find out.

She pulled Jack's cell phone from her bag. He'd never allowed her to have one, but he'd always had the latest, most expensive phone available. He'd told her it was to "manage their affairs," but she knew now that meant pornography and online poker.

She rarely touched the thing and only carried it now because she knew Jack would hate the thought of her using it. She tapped the phone icon, her fingers trembling as she dialed the number, and raised the phone to her ear. Her spirits soared as she heard the tones of a ringing phone.

"Orison Industries, how may I direct your call?"

"Oh, hello," Moira stammered. She truly hadn't expected to reach anyone. "I'm calling about your job advertisement for the switchboard operator position. Is it—"

"Please hold."

After a brief interlude of lively fiddle music, a warm female voice said, "This is Iris, how can I help you?"

"My name is Mrs. Moira Sullivan, and I'm calling in reference to the switchboard operator position. I'd be very interested in applying if the position is still open, Ms.—"

"Iris," the woman repeated. "And yes, the position is still open. It's been incredibly challenging to find an appropriate candidate."

"I can imagine," Moira said, her spirits buoyed. "You know, I actually have experience as a PBX switchboard operator. I'd love the opportunity to interview."

"That's wonderful," Iris replied. "Could you come in this afternoon, say three o'clock?"

Moira glanced up at wall clock in the lobby. Her eyes widened as she read the time—almost fifteen after two. That should be enough time to get downtown on the bus, but she'd be cutting it close. They must be in quite a hurry to fill the position, and if that was the case, they'd probably be more inclined to give her a chance. So why not give it a try? If it didn't work out, there was always Plan B.

"Of course."

"Wonderful. Do you know the Crawford building downtown? It's at the intersection of 8th and Broad."

"Why yes, I do. I used to work there many years ago." Moira paused, searching her memory. "But I thought… Hasn't it been empty since the late 90s? The city was talking about demolishing it not long ago."

"We've always been here," Iris said. "We don't advertise our presence. I suppose we're old-fashioned that way."

"I'm a bit old-fashioned myself."

Moira heard the sound of a phone ringing in the background. "I'm so sorry, I have another call," Iris said, "but I look forward to seeing you here at three. I'll meet you in the lobby."

Moira ended the call, overcome by a feeling somewhere between wonderment and disbelief. She thought, and not for the first time, she might be losing her mind. There was plenty of evidence to support the idea. For one thing, she saw her dead husband Jack in mirrors and heard him talking to her—*at* her, really. At first, she'd thought the house was the problem. They'd lived there for fifty years, it made sense that Jack's presence would linger there. So she'd sold the house and moved into a tiny apartment in a senior living community, only for him to follow her. She'd covered every mirror in the place the day after moving in. That had helped some, but she could still hear him behind the cloth, grousing at her.

And now, in her darkest hour, her dream job turned up. A job that would take her back to the best days of her life, the days before Jack. A job that should no longer exist but miraculously did—and in the very building she'd worked in. It was, now that she thought about it, all a bit much. But this new delusion held the promise of happiness, while the rest of her life promised only more pain, more humiliation, more suffering, more *Jack*. She might as well see where it took her.

Moira tapped the search bar on the screen of Jack's phone.

"Okay, Google," she said, putting her "Phone Skills for Seniors" class to use. "Find a bus route to 8th and Broad."

The bus bumped to a halt one block north of the Crawford building. Moira levered herself out of her seat and navigated the aisle to the front of the bus. She was grateful it was almost empty, and she didn't have to step over outstretched legs. When she'd worked here in the 60s, the bus had always been crowded with commuters and tourists in the summer. Now, the only other people on the bus were the driver and a sleeping man, probably homeless and taking advantage of the air conditioning. She slowly made her way down the steep steps of the bus onto the sidewalk. The doors folded shut behind her. With a squeal, the bus lurched into motion and pulled away, leaving her in the baking afternoon heat.

It broke her heart to see how downtown had changed. When she'd worked here, the storefronts had all been occupied by local businesses. A pharmacy with a soda fountain, a hardware store, a candy shop—now, they all stood empty.

Moira checked her watch. 2:53. She'd better get going. She didn't want to be late for her imaginary job interview. She laughed out loud, startling herself. Oh, yes… it was quite possible that she was losing her mind.

The Crawford building looked abandoned. The stone façade sported graffiti and what looked like a scattering of bullet holes. The plate glass windows were dark and dusty. Moira rattled both handles of the double doors. They were, as she'd feared, locked, but before she turned to walk away, the grand revolving door caught her attention.

She stepped into the open partition and pushed. The door glided smoothly, and she exited into the lobby of days gone by. Moira's mouth gaped open in disbelief. The lobby was brightly lit by a huge crystal chandelier, just as she remembered. The tile floors were waxed to a glossy sheen, and the scent of multiple fresh floral arrangements filled the space. The only difference between what she saw now and what she'd seen every workday from 1962 until 1968 was the lack of people.

The sharp clack of a woman's heels striking the tile floor belied the impression of emptiness, and Moira turned to see a slim figure striding briskly toward her. She was immediately struck by her hair, which was—though she appeared to be in her early 30s—as white as snow, styled in a chin-length flipped bob with side swept bangs. Her sky blue, boatneck sheath dress was paired with a slim white ribbon belt and low-heeled Mary Jane pumps. She could have stepped right out of the pages of a 1962 Ladies Home Journal.

"You must be Mrs. Sullivan," she said, extending her hand. "It's such a pleasure to meet you."

"It's very nice to meet you as well, Mrs...." Moira waited for the woman to supply her surname. When the pause stretched too long, she said, "I'm sorry, I didn't catch your last name."

"Just call me Iris," the woman said, taking Moira's hand with surprising gentleness. "I'm like Liberace, I only use the one name." A dazzling smile lit up her face.

"It's a pleasure to meet you, Iris," she said. "And please, call me Moira."

Iris released her hand and turned, gesturing toward the bank of elevators at the rear of the lobby. "Shall we?"

Moira followed her across the lobby, marveling at how little change time had wrought over the past fifty years. It truly was remarkable. Iris pressed the button to call the elevator, and the doors immediately opened with a chime. She stepped into the carpeted car and gestured for Moira to follow. Moira glanced into the elevator and froze, staring at the mirrored walls with dread.

Jack.

Moira cleared her throat. "Iris," she said, "would you mind terribly if I took the stairs and met you at the top?"

Iris smiled warmly, but shook her head. "I'm sorry, but I have you sandwiched into the only open space in my calendar. Time,

I'm afraid, is of the essence." The elevator chimed again, and the doors began to close. Iris pressed a button and they jolted open. "Our office is in the penthouse, and it would be quite a long climb. Do come in."

Moira gritted her teeth and stepped into the elevator. As she'd feared, Jack's face loomed large in each of the three mirrored walls. He leered appreciatively at Iris, who was leaning forward to press the button marked PH.

Now that's *what a woman ought to look like. Look at you, old and withered. I don't think you were ever young and alive like this. You were an old maid on our wedding day.*

Moira squeezed her eyes shut as a bead of sweat dripped down her temple. She just had to make it through this elevator ride. How long could it possibly take? Thirty seconds? She'd lived with Jack for fifty years; she could handle that. She opened her eyes and squared her shoulders, focusing on the hum of the elevator and the sensation of rising. She could do this.

"Are you all right, Moira?"

She turned to Iris, forcing a pleasant smile onto her face. "Oh, yes," she said. "Just a bit nervous. This is only my second job interview in the past fifty years."

Jack howled with laughter. *You haven't had a job since that girl's mother was born! Give it up, Mo. You're used up and worn out, practically dead. Especially next to a fine piece of—*

"Excuse me," Iris said. "But you have a little something... I hope you don't mind."

Before Moira could react, she reached over and, with a feather light touch, swept her fingertips over Moira's eyes, which fluttered closed. Moira felt a pulling sensation in the center of her forehead, followed by a subtle snap.

"There," Iris said. "Much better."

Moira opened her eyes. She felt… well, she couldn't find the right word. Unburdened? Liberated?

Revived.

It was like she'd been seeing the world in black and white and, all of a sudden, the colors returned in a blooming spectrum of beauty. Jack was gone. He was *gone.* She couldn't see him in any of the mirrors. Even better, she couldn't feel him. Tears flooded her eyes, and she pressed one hand to trembling lips.

"Thank you," Moira breathed. "Oh, thank you." Who *was* this woman? How had she done… whatever it was she had done? Was this all part of an elaborate psychosis?

It didn't matter. Jack was *gone.*

She opened her mouth to ask Iris to explain, but the elevator's chime sounded and the doors glided open. Iris stepped out of the elevator and extended her right arm gracefully, gesturing for Moira to follow.

They entered a reception area flooded with afternoon sun from the floor-to-ceiling windows. In lieu of curtains, dozens of prisms of different shapes and sizes hung from the curtain rod, suspended on slim gold chains. The light refracting through the prisms created rainbows on the walls and the terrazzo floor. Moira stood transfixed for a moment, but the brisk tapping of Iris's heels broke the spell.

Iris had turned down a broad hallway with an open door at the end. Moira, still a bit giddy from the sudden departure of Jack's vitriolic spirit, squinted after her silhouette and followed. Iris entered the office at the end of the hall and swept across the room, taking a seat behind a white lacquer desk. With a wave of her hand, she invited Moira to take the seat across from her. The room was otherwise empty. No phone, no photographs or knickknacks, no art on the walls. Yet somehow, the space did not feel bare. It was flooded with light, open and spacious, comforting in the way a cat might feel lying in a sunbeam.

"I'm delighted you were able to come in on such short notice," Iris said. "As I mentioned, we've had a terrible time trying to fill this position. The world has moved on, I suppose."

"Everything's about computers these days," Moira said. "I know things are more efficient that way, but it feels so impersonal. There's a craftsmanship to the old-fashioned ways, I think." She opened her leather portfolio and pulled out the heavy sheet of paper on which she'd carefully typed her résumé. "Here's an example for you." She placed the paper on Iris's desk. "The last interviewer who saw this was utterly horrified that I used an electric typewriter."

"I wish I still had mine," Iris said.

Moira couldn't imagine the woman was old enough to have ever used one. Still, she leaned forward and said, "You can find them on Amazon. They're a bit pricey, but if you're a luddite like me, it's well worth the expense."

Iris picked up the résumé, scanning the document as she

spoke. "Using a typewriter certainly requires a level of attention to detail not often seen today."

Moira watched her face for any sign of a reaction.

"Very impressive, Moira. You have exactly the kind of experience we've been searching for."

Moira's spirits soared. "I'm so glad to hear that."

Iris replaced the résumé on her desk, nudging the page until it was centered precisely on the lacquered white surface. She looked up at Moira, holding her gaze until the pause stretched to the brink of discomfort. "You'll find that I'm a rather unconventional interviewer," she said. "I make most of my decisions based on more... esoteric criteria than experience or education. I believe that the right candidate can be trained to the requirements of the job. The more important qualifications relate to character, to temperament, to the condition of the soul."

"The soul?"

"Yes," Iris said. "The soul. I know it sounds like spiritual mumbo jumbo, but I hope my meaning will become clear as the interview progresses." She smiled at Moira. "Can you bear with my quirks?"

This woman had gotten rid of Jack. Moira felt like she could bear with just about anything. "Of course."

"I have only three primary interview questions," Iris said. "Though I may ask you to clarify and expand upon your answers. Your responses to these questions will tell me all I need to know."

"That sounds easy enough."

"Before we begin, may I offer you a glass of water?" She

gestured toward a narrow table against the far wall of the office. A short, round clay pitcher rested on a silver tray in the center of the table, its handle arching high above the lip. The vessel had a glossy black background, against which a winged woman had been painted in gold. In one of her hands, the woman held a staff; in the other, she held a pitcher much like the one upon which she was featured. Two small stemmed glasses sat next to the pitcher.

Moira would have sworn on a stack of Bibles that the table hadn't been there when she came in, but it had been a very strange day. Her observational skills were, perhaps, not at their best. Either way, she was anxious to get to the meat of the interview, and she wasn't particularly thirsty.

"Oh, no," Moira said. "I'm fine." She was getting nervous again.

"Oh, but I insist," Iris said. "A cool glass of water on a hot day like this is so refreshing."

She crossed the room and retrieved the tray. Sliding Moira's résumé to the side, she placed the tray on the desk. She sat down and cupped the bowl of the pitcher in her hands, closing her eyes. Her lips moved as though she was speaking a few words. Before Moira could decide whether she should close her eyes too—perhaps for some kind of prayer—the moment had passed, and Iris was lifting the pitcher. She poured the water slowly and with great ceremony. It reminded Moira of a Japanese tea ceremony she'd once seen in a movie.

Iris lifted one glass with both hands and passed it to Moira, then raised her own glass. "I've always felt that honesty is the bedrock of any fruitful relationship," she said. "Shall we drink to truth?"

"To truth," Moira echoed. She drank deeply, draining her cup. The water was cold, much colder than she'd anticipated given the lack of ice. It felt heavy in her mouth and throat, plummeting to the pit of her stomach with an unexpected weight. She felt the cold spreading through her body, radiating down into her legs, out into her arms, tingling up to the crown of her head. Her mind slowed and sharpened, crystallizing like frost on a windowpane.

"I feel… strange."

The words formed slowly, drop by drop, like icicles after a winter storm. Moira carefully replaced the cup on the desk before her numb hands could drop it.

"All is well," Iris said, and patted her hand. "Let's get through these questions, shall we? It won't take long." She placed the glasses on the tray and slid it to the edge of the desk so there was nothing between her and Moira. "Now." She rested her clasped hands on the desk. "What do you offer?"

What an odd question. Moira supposed she was asking about her previous experience, so she prepared to launch into a description of the skills she'd used as a switchboard operator—customer service, diligence, attention to detail. But that wasn't what actually came out of her mouth.

"Endurance." Her eyes widened, but her mouth continued. "No matter the trial, I have endured."

Where on earth had that come from?

"Excellent," Iris said. She jotted a note on a sheet of paper that most definitely had not been there a few seconds ago. "Let's move on to my second question. What do you wish to earn?"

They were going to discuss salary already? Moira had no idea what reasonable compensation for a position like this would be these days.

"Redemption." Moira snapped her mouth shut, biting off the end of the word. Something was wrong with her.

"Why do you need redemption?"

"I killed my husband, Jack," Moira said. Her voice was calm, matter of fact, but her mind was roiling. Why was she saying such things?

"This would be the charming man I rid you of in the elevator?"

Moira opened her mouth to ask how Iris had done it, how she'd gotten rid of him. Instead, she simply said, "Yes."

"He seemed like the kind of man who sucked the air right out of a room." Iris leaned back in her chair. "My own husband is a bit of a blowhard, but he's not a cruel man, not like your Jack." She cocked her head and looked at Moira. "He abused you, didn't he?"

"Yes." As she spoke, she felt the sting of that first slap all over again. That had been Jack's weapon of choice, the backhanded slap. He'd said to her many times that he'd never *hit* a woman, but he'd sure as hell slap some sense into one.

"You killed him to stop the abuse?"

"No." She commanded her body to stand up, to get up and walk right out of this room, but she continued to sit, placid, hands folded on her lap.

"Why did you kill him?"

Moira pressed her lips together. It wasn't too late. She could stop this before it went any further. She could say that she'd meant something different, not that she'd literally ended Jack's life. But even thinking about lying made the feeling of cold and heaviness inside her grow. More than that, it felt obscene, grotesque, especially considering the reason she'd done it.

"He lied to me," Moira said. Icy tears welled up, spilling over and streaking down her cheeks. "I always wanted children. Before we were married, he told me he wanted them too. He promised we'd have a family, and we tried to have a baby for years. He was always *happy* to try," she said. Her bitter heart burned with the cold truth. "As time passed, Jack said it must not be God's will for us to be parents." Her breath hitched with a repressed sob. *Don't say another word.*

"Go on."

"He was sick at the end," Moira said. "Very sick. Emphysema and lung cancer. He smoked a pack a day for more than fifty years, but he wouldn't stop—not even when he was dying. We started getting calls from collection agencies. He told me it must be a mistake, but I thought with his illness, he might have missed something. I went through his files—he kept everything, prescription receipts, doctor's bills, insurance claims, everything. I found..."

She could not go on. She couldn't bear it.

"What did you find, Moira?"

"I found a record from 1968, just a month before we were married." She clenched her fists. The anger she'd felt on that day came flooding back, only instead of feeling like molten lava in her veins as it had then, it felt like a glacier tearing through her heart.

"He had a vasectomy." Her voice broke on the word. She was choking on unshed tears. "Before we were married, before we ever… before we started trying, he had a vasectomy. He watched my hopes rise and be crushed, month after month, for years." The glacier dug a deep furrow through the center of her being. "I put up with him, with how he treated me, because when it came to this, he was always so gentle with me."

Moira fell silent. Surely, this was enough. Iris watched her, waiting.

"I didn't just look at the medical paperwork," she said. "I also went through our finances. Over the last five years, he spent everything we had on video poker and women who do… things on cameras over the internet." The words were coming faster and faster now. She no longer wanted to stop. "He knew he was going to die, and he wanted to leave me with nothing. He broke his promise. He took motherhood from me." She slammed her palms flat on the table. "He took fifty years of my life!"

The sound echoed through the room. Iris did not react. She simply watched and waited.

"It was strange," Moira said. "I didn't cry when I found out. I didn't yell at him. I didn't even tell him that I knew." The terrible pressure in her chest was easing. "I had a prescription for sleeping pills, and I put three of them into his last drink of the night. After he fell asleep, I put a pillow over his face. I held it there until I was sure he was dead. He hardly struggled at all."

Moira stared down at her hands, the hands that had taken Jack's life. The cold, heavy feeling had dissipated. She felt more in control of herself, but having come this far, she wanted to finish.

"I thought about confessing when the ambulance came," she said. "I prayed the prayer I always come back to when I don't know what else to do. 'Thy will be done.' If the police had asked if I killed him, I would have told them. But no one ever asked. And here I am, a free woman. A murderer."

"Thy will be done," Iris repeated. "That and 'thank you' are the only prayers anyone ever needs."

They sat in silence for a moment. Moira waited for the words she knew she'd hear. *I'll need to notify the police.* She wouldn't fight it. She just wanted it to be over. But Iris didn't speak. She stood and crossed the room to the large window, looking down on the derelict and nearly deserted neighborhood below. She turned to face Moira, silhouetted against the window.

"I have only one more question for you," she said. "Here at Orison Industries, we serve the Great Work of this world." The light in the room changed, brightening perceptibly. Moira squinted at Iris, struggling to make sense of what she was seeing. "We answer humanity's greatest and most fundamental need. The people who work here, who serve this mission, must be completely and unfailingly dedicated." Brilliant white light glowed from Iris's skin, refracting into rainbows as though shining through a prism.

"Will you serve, Moira?" There was a rush of displaced air, as two great golden wings unfurled behind her. "Will you give your life to the Great Work?"

All Moira's fears and uncertainties, her guilt and her shame, fell away as she stood. She'd never been sure about anything in her life. Jack had refused to play board games with her because she always dithered so long when it was her turn. Not this time. This time, she knew. This was why she was here, why she'd endured the pain and humiliation and aching loneliness of her life. Every experience she'd had was leading up to this moment, shaping her into the person she needed to be.

"I will."

At her words, the light flared, blotting out the room in a wash of pure white. Her eyes closed involuntarily, and a wave of dizziness swept over her. The sound of a great wind rushed past her ears. She felt a sense of movement, of rising, but no air moved across her skin. She reached for the edge of the desk to steady herself, but it was gone.

The sound faded, replaced by the murmur of female voices coming from somewhere behind her. Moira opened her eyes to find herself seemingly floating in a sea of white. She could feel the floor underneath her, but when she peered down anxiously, all she saw was her sensible shoes against what looked like an unbroken expanse of snow. Everything everywhere was just... white. Had she had a stroke? Was she dead?

"Moira?"

She turned and saw Iris standing in front of a row of three high-back switchboards. The chairs in front of the left and middle stations were occupied by two women; the chair on the right was vacant. It was their voices she heard. The switchboards looked just as she remembered them. The back panel was lined with rows of female jacks, each labeled and paired with an indicator light. The operator's table held columns of toggle switches, more lights, and a bank of cords. Moira took a step toward the empty chair. She wanted nothing more than to sit down and run her fingers over the switches, to examine the cords and labels.

"Moira," Iris repeated. "I know the rainbow bridge can be disorienting, but I need your attention."

With a great deal of effort, Moira pulled her eyes away from the switchboards.

Iris stepped toward Moira and took both of her hands. "I'd like to offer you a permanent post at the switchboard." Moira opened her mouth to accept, but Iris cut her off. "I need to explain what the job requires and what your duties will be before you make your decision." She stepped back and gestured toward the women at the switchboards, who continued to answer and route calls. "Orison Industries employs three operators, each with different spheres of responsibility. I'll introduce you to your colleagues momentarily. I trust you're familiar with operating this type of switchboard?"

"Yes," Moira said. "I used one just like it at the insurance company. I do have a question, though."

"Ask."

"I just realized that I have no idea what Orison Industries does," Moira said. "I should have researched the company before I came to the interview, but it all happened so quickly."

"I know it's been an overwhelming day," Iris said. "All will be explained, I promise. Let's start with meeting your coworkers. I'll let them explain what we do here at Orison." She stepped between the two women and laid one hand on each of their shoulders. "Ladies," she said, "could you take a break and meet your new counterpart?"

The women removed their headsets and rose to greet her. Both of them wore mirrored aviator sunglasses. Moira was a bit taken aback, but it was bright in here, and this small detail was far and away one of the lesser marvels of the day. The woman who'd been seated on the far left stepped forward. She was young, maybe in her early twenties, and olive-skinned. Her long hair hung in ringlets down her back, crowned with a wreath of flowers. She wore a flowing white dress, bound tightly under the breast and flowing over the swell of her belly.

"I'm Nona," she said, smiling. "It's a pleasure to meet you."

"And my name is Decima," the other woman said, an exotic lilt coloring her words. Her black hair was pulled into a high topknot, which was wrapped in strands of cinnabar beads. She wore a draped dress in brilliant turquoise, and her dark skin was radiant with health and life. She took both of Moira's hands in hers. "I am delighted to meet you. We've been waiting so long to welcome a third sister."

"I'm happy to meet you, too," Moira said. She looked at Nona. "And it appears congratulations are in order. Is this your first baby?"

"Thank you," Nona said, with a gracious nod. "And no, not

my first. I have many children. Motherhood is my true calling."

Moira's heart ached at that, but Nona was almost archetypically fertile, sunlight and spring and new life. It seemed somehow right that she had borne many children. Moira, on the other hand, had apparently been made for darker duties.

"What do you do here?" she asked. "What kind of calls do you take?"

"We answer prayers," Decima said.

"Prayers?"

"Yes," Nona said. "Prayers. We each have our own areas of expertise. I handle petitions regarding the springtime of life—beginnings, growth." She laughed and cradled her belly. "Pregnancy and babies."

"I am responsible for the concerns of mid-life, the summertime of the soul," Decima said. "Marriage and parenthood, but also success, ambition, and striving."

"Then I," Moira said, "must be fall and winter. Death and dying, justice and retribution."

Iris nodded. "You understand." She gestured toward the switchboards, inviting the women to take their seats. "Calls are pre-sorted and routed to you for resolution. On occasion, you may get a call best handled by one of your colleagues, which you can simply transfer via the switchboard." She gestured to the jacks for the other stations. "Your primary duty is to determine whether the caller's concern should be routed Upstairs for resolution."

"I decide whether the prayer will be answered," Moira said.

"Yes."

"All the prayers of the world?"

"Yes."

"But there are billions of people alive now, not to mention all of those who have come before and who will come after."

"This is a timeless place," Nona said. "There is no before, no after."

"Once you are here, you have *always* been here," Decima said.

"But who am I to decide which prayers should be answered?" Moira shook her head. "I'm not God."

"No," Iris said. "You are not God. You decide in accordance with The Plan."

Iris walked to the side of the switchboard. A sealed envelope hung from a magnetic clip. She retrieved it and handed it to Moira. It was thin and light, but it tugged at Moira's senses with the weight of a trillion lifetimes. She carefully slid her finger under the flap and broke the wax seal. She paused and looked up at Iris.

"You've read it?"

"No," Iris said. "The Plan is not for me. Only the Fates and the Almighty can bear the knowledge of it."

Moira nodded. She hesitated before removing the page from the envelope. This was the point of no return. She knew, deep down, that she could still walk out of here if she chose. Her fate was not sealed until she read this document. She carefully slid the sheet of paper out, just one sheet for the fate of an entire universe, and unfolded it. She scanned it once, then read it again, slowly. As she read, her eyes began to glow, the luminescence growing and growing until her eyes were pools of brilliant white light. When she looked up, she saw that Nona and Decima had removed their sunglasses. Their eyes shone like newborn stars.

"I understand everything," Moira said. A smile played on her lips, a smile born in a heart that had finally found peace. "The pain, the suffering, the unanswered prayers… I couldn't be this," she said, gesturing toward the switchboard, "if I had never been that. It all serves a higher purpose."

"It all serves The Plan," Decima said. She slipped her headset on and plugged a jack into the board to answer the call.

"*We* serve The Plan," Nona said, smiling like sunrise. She turned her attention to the array of flickering lights before her.

Moira donned her own headset, adjusting the fit until it was just right. She looked at the switchboard before her, feeling a deep and profound sense of rightness, of belonging, of Fate.

"Everything serves The Plan."

BLONDES NEED NOT APPLY

By Autumn Shah

THE KOHL LINER TUGS the tender skin under Miriam's eye. Her sister's face looms in hers, the tip of her tongue revealing her concentration.

She wants to complain about the burning sensation, but she fights the urge and focuses on the Vesta Tilley song playing on the Victrola in the other room. It isn't often her older sisters want to spend time with her, let alone allow her to be the center of their attention.

"Miriam, you moved again!" Lenore says.

Miriam doesn't reply, afraid even moving her lips in defense will arouse her sister's anger and cause her to call the whole production off.

Lenore uses her fingers to smudge the kohl further under her eye and out into the creases. She stands and examines her handiwork. "And now for lipstick."

"Let me do it," Louise says, snatching the lipstick before

Lenore can. "I'm better at this part."

Miriam notices a streak of rouge on Louise's frock and wonders if she should warn her about it before Mother sees. She decides against it, as Louise can afford a moment in their mother's bad graces, whereas Miriam, and certainly Lenore—the one most often in the soup with their mother—cannot.

Father had been the first to see the notice in yesterday morning's Peabody Gazette, right under the advertisement for W.B. Cyclist Corsets:

DO YOU HAVE THE LOOK?
VAMP LOOK-ALIKE BEAUTY PAGEANT

WEDNESDAY, AUGUST 22ND
CRAWFORD GYMNASIUM
SPECIAL APPEARANCE AND FINAL JUDGING BY
THE VAMP HERSELF...THEDA BARA!!

BLONDES NEED NOT APPLY

All of Kansas knew the famous actress would be passing through Florence on her way to California, finishing a promotional tour for her latest film, *Cleopatra*. And now she was stopping in this rinky-dink town of theirs? And judging a beauty contest of girls trying to look like her? This would be the most excitement Florence had seen this century.

It hadn't occurred to Miriam to enter. Her sisters were the pretty ones. They were so blonde the sunlight seemed to follow them around. Their blue eyes matched their mother's, and the three of them were constantly commented upon; "the blonde Beckers."

When Miriam was born with dark hair and a swarthier skin color, she was said to take after her great-grandmother on her father's side, a Spanish Jewess, and she was given a Jewess name suitable enough for an Episcopalian.

Lenore was the one who came up with the batty idea of entering Miriam in the contest. At first, Miriam wanted nothing to do with it.

"That's a load of hooey. I'm not getting all dolled up and standing on a stage in front of a hundred people," Miriam had said.

"She's right," Louise said. "Can you see Miriam dressed up, walking in high heels and twirling pearls?"

"It's not as if either of us could pull it off," Lenore said. "Don't you want to meet Theda Bara?"

"I do!" Mother said, as she walked in carrying Father's toast. "And I think Miriam would absolutely be able to sashay across a stage in pearls or a feather boa." Mother mimed twirling a long boa with her free hand and the three girls laughed.

Father put an arm around Mother's waist to draw her—and his toast—closer.

"Maybe your mother should get up there, all dressed up like a movie star."

Mother set down his toast and spun out of his grasp.

"If Blanche Sweet or Billie Burke were judging a look-alike

contest, maybe!"

"That's right, Miriam. Dark hair and eyes are all the rage," Louise said. "A little mascara and we can really play up those eyes of yours and turn you into 'a sultry vamp who always gets her man!'"

The three girls crowded around Father's open newspaper, a flurry of ideas passing between them.

"Alright, that's enough," Father said half-heartedly, slipping his newspaper onto his lap. "No daughter of mine is going to parade around in public half-dressed looking like a-a-"

"A har—"

Father held up his hand to stop what was about to come out of Lenore's mouth.

Lenore pursed her lips and clasped her hands behind her.

"Geoffrey, no one will be parading around half-dressed," Mother said from the kitchen doorway. "I'll make sure of it." She walked up behind Father and put her hands on his shoulders. "Imagine, we'll have a chance to see the great vamp herself!"

Father rolled his eyes and shifted in his seat. "Some of us have to work, so you'll just have to give Bara my regards when you see her."

Father pushed away from the table, and Mother gave the girls a look of suppressed excitement.

The girls knew very well the story of Mother and her first film.

She was nineteen and had just met their father. It so happened, the night of their first date, Mr. Frank Goff and his black tent and projector came to town selling tickets for five cents to see his moving pictures.

"Well, it was truly some kind of magic! I remember grasping your father's hand and holding so tight. But I couldn't tell you if it was out of fear, or excitement! And, oh! Annabelle Butterfly Dance! It was the most amazing minute of my life up to that point."

From that time on, she'd followed everything to do with films and pored over every issue of *Motion Picture Story* and *Photoplay* magazines that Father allowed her to purchase each month. She was besotted with the actresses and their real lives off the celluloid. She had her favorites; Madge Evans, Virginia Pearson. But there hadn't been anyone like Theda Bara before.

It was in the dark of the morning, leaving Kansas City, Missouri when I was told the train would make a stop in Florence, Kansas so I could judge yet another vamp beauty pageant. I decide to go back to reading my Buchan novel.

Chass squirms in my lap and I stroke his tawny fur, scratch his folded black ears.

"Alright, Monsieur Chassinat. Let's get up for a walkie then."

Recognizing the word, he springs off my lap and turns circles at my feet.

I set my book down and look over at my mother, still asleep on her folded-out berth. This is her first trip out to California, and I am excited to show her warm sand and palm trees.

I stand up, flattening down my skirt in the back, and pull down my waistcoat. I feel around for the leash in my open valise. We have a compartment to ourselves, and Chass certainly has a bit of room to wander in, considering his small size. Yet he has been bouncing around the cabin, chasing shadows and licking corners, much to my mother's chagrin.

I clip the leash and quietly unlatch the door. Chass slides out as soon as the door is wide enough.

A porter stands close by, presumably waiting for his assigned passengers to awaken.

"Mornin', Miss Bara," he says.

"Good morning. Could you have coffee and pastries sent?"

"Sure thing," he says, turning in the direction of the dining car.

Chass tugs on the leash as I pause to shut the door gently behind me, and we set off down the hallway toward the observation car.

Out the windows, the sun is rising, and I see yellow, late summer grass and tall cornfields and the occasional farmhouse in the distance. I love train travel. I love being rocked to sleep. I love being trapped with nothing to do but read. And I love seeing parts of our great country that are a mystery to so many.

These towns aren't so different from the ones outside Cincinnati, where I grew up. But I've been instructed by my publicity men not to relate to the locals. After all, I am supposed to be the daughter of French and Italian artists, born "in the shadow of the Sphinx." I am mysterious. I bedeck my home in furs and crystal balls and am endowed with a wisdom that comes from that Eastern lineage.

In truth, I am the least exotic person one could imagine. Out of my snake bra and bejeweled gowns, I am quite frumpy, I admit. I prefer quilts—stitched by the Quakers back home—over tiger skins, and brocade curtains over sheer silk. I travel with my mother and sister and sometimes my younger brother, not a bevy of lusty men. I don't think I've left a single man pining after me, except, perhaps one who imagined himself in love with one of my characters.

I find it all quite laughable on the surface. But if I dwell on it, it's unsettling to be deemed something you are so far from, and don't aspire in the least to be. I just wanted to be an actor. I didn't know that my persona would be a clever publicity stunt that would continue to hang over me like a gossamer veil.

The observation car is bright with morning sun shining in from the large windows on both sides of the car. I spend half my day here when I'm traveling alone. Mother doesn't like the direct sun, nor does she appreciate the way the light throws as the train takes turns this way and that, making her woozy.

There are a few early risers, like myself, milling about. I let Chass down and keep his leash taut. Passengers are used to my presence and I get tips of the hat and smiles as I walk through to the back of the car.

I open the door to the outside and Chass helps lead me through, excited by the moving air and outside smells. There is no one else on the platform, so I take my preference of the three chairs screwed into the floor. Chass dashes from one side of the small platform to the other, sticking his nose through the railing and barking at cows or the occasional pedestrian walking by the tracks. The train shimmies back and forth, rocking me into a trance. I am being hastened forward by the power of steam, but my gaze holds fast to the tracks as they grow longer and ever more distant.

The first Theda Bara film Miriam had been allowed to see was *The Two Orphans*. She hadn't been very compelled by the story of the rich girl and her sister who find themselves suddenly orphaned and endangered. And she didn't think the actress her mother loved so much was very convincing as a young girl.

Besides, Miriam found herself frustrated much of the time; there were never enough subtitles for her to fully understand what was going on in any given scene. Louise accused her of having too little imagination when she complained about it.

Miriam was more fascinated by the five-piece orchestra that often played along with the films. She craned her neck to see the bows of the violinists sliding back and forth, their cheeks pressed against their instruments in adoration. It seemed to her there was a love story playing out right there in the orchestra pit. More often though, there was a single organist playing music that floated through Miriam's chest and seemed to lift up out of her again. The lady organist at the Mayflower Theater was her favorite. Miriam loved to watch her. She was a young woman, Miriam guessed. She barely looked at the keys her fingers moved across because her face was turned to the screen, her expressions mirroring those of the actors telling the story.

By the time Miriam saw *Sin* and then *Carmen*, she was of an age to understand what set Theda Bara apart from other actresses. Theda Bara held her audience enrapt with a multitude of conflicting emotions in a single glance. She was one of those women who every other woman wanted to be, but was also a little afraid of. Miriam wondered if she would grow up to be like that. She didn't quite know how one obtained that quality, or where it led, but she knew it was a quality that could be useful.

Miriam had no aspirations to be an actress. She had no confidence in her ability to hide what she might be feeling or express what she did not. But a little mystery or notoriety would be amusing for a while. She was largely left to her own devices as the youngest in a house of busy women with their own interests, activities and lives. She often felt insignificant beside her angelic-looking sisters who she so wished to be closer with. The prospect of this beauty pageant had lifted her into a position of more importance than she'd previously enjoyed in her family, and her body hummed under their attention.

As Louise's fingers rub rouge onto Miriam's upper cheekbones, their mother rummages through her closet looking for something appropriate for a fourteen-almost-fifteen-year old to wear, yet that still bears the quality of a motion picture siren.

"Look to the right a bit," Louise tells Miriam. She turns her head slightly.

"To the right, I said!"

Miriam sticks her tongue out at her sister, who either ignores or doesn't see the swift gesture.

Just then Mother emerges from the closet. "Girls, I think I found something that will work perfectly."

She drapes the clothes over the bed rail then holds up a belted, sequined chemise.

"Alright, let's see how this goes on." She motions to Miriam.

Miriam hops off the stool and stands before her mother in her pale pink slip. She holds her arms up so her mother can slip the sleeveless dress over her head.

"It's too long," Lenore moans.

"Actually, it might work," Mother says, as she loosens the sash. "I've seen the dresses in the magazines having a drop waist"—she ties the sash again at Miriam's hips and gives the dress a tug from the bottom—"just like this."

"She can wear the ruched pantaloons underneath," Lenore says, pulling them out from under some of the other garments draped over the rail.

"Or, I have that black lace skirt," Louise says.

Lenore shakes her head. "The pants will look more modern."

"Either would look lovely," says Mother, smiling into Miriam's face, warming her all over.

"We could borrow Aunt May's black feather boa!" Louise suggests.

"What about her hair?" Lenore asks. "She should wear it down."

Mother tucks Miriam's hair behind her ears. "What do you

think, dear? How do you want to wear your hair?" She turns her around to face the mirror.

Miriam is bashful staring into the mirror with her sisters and Mother watching. She turns away, but her mother holds her there, standing in the reflection with her. Mother fluffs the dark curls and tucks one side behind her ear. "Maybe a little setting here?"

Miriam nods.

"Theda Bara is going to wonder why you're not the one on the screen."

She blushes so that she feels she must not need the rouge just applied.

"Because of you, we're going to get to meet Theda Bara!" Lenore jumps up and down.

Miriam grins, happy to be the harbinger of excitement.

"Really, Miriam, you're going to knock 'em dead! Bara will probably ask you to go to California with her," Louise says. "You'd better pack your bags!"

"When you get to California, make sure you tell everyone about your dear mother, and that I'm happy to play maids, mothers or shopkeepers," Mother says, patting the back of her own fashionably short, curled bob.

"Yes, you'll bring us all to California and we'll finally see the ocean!"

"And Wally Reid! Maybe you'll marry Wally, Miriam!"

"Come now, stop," Mother says. "We've gone on with this silliness long enough. Besides, Wally is much too old for Miriam."

"Oh, Mother, you just want him for yourself," Lenore says.

"Shh... Don't let your father hear that!" Mother winks.

The girls laugh, including Miriam, who is now imagining herself, and Wallace Reid on the beach. He'd have his hair slicked back, wearing a suit and bow tie and that playful grin...

Her mind is awhirl with myriad thoughts. What if she is chosen by Theda? How should she react? What should she say? If she wins, would it really mean she'd get to go to California? Maybe this was the direction her life was supposed to take. Her sisters both have their lives planned out. Louise wants to marry Jacob Dunmore and have lots of children and design hats. Lenore plans to go to nursing school because she doesn't mind the sight of blood and their father told them that soon wounded troops would be coming home from the war and need to be taken care of.

Miriam doesn't have anything like that. Maybe this will be the moment that leads to the rest of her life.

My mother is up and arranging her hair in the small mirror when Chass and I return to our compartment.

"Good morning, Mother."

She had put on a loose-fitting summer dress over the silk cami-knickers she wore to bed.

"How you get up and about so early, I'll never understand," she says.

Chass jumps up on the cushioned bench and plops his

haunches down beside my book, waiting for me to sit.

"We didn't wake you, did we?"

"No, dear. I'm only teasing you," she says, turning from the mirror. "You were ever a busy bee, up and at 'em before the rest of the world."

"Mother, I do hope you like it in California."

"I'm sure I'll like it just fine," she says, taking her small valise from under the berth.

"No, I mean really like it. You see, I'm going to have to move out here." There, I said it. I'd been waiting for the right time. "It's where the film industry is headed. Anyone who's anyone is already on their way to living in Los Angeles and Burbank…"

"I expected as much." She sits on the bench behind the small, fold-out table that holds two cups of steaming coffee and some pastries.

"I'd like you to move there with me."

"And what does your sister say?"

It irks me that she knows I already talked to Lori. "She said she'll come."

She chooses a pastry and gently elbows Chass aside when he approaches. I am asking her to move across the country, to leave her life behind.

"Well, what does your crystal ball predict?"

I laugh and finally sit down beside her. The crystal ball is a joke between us. I had "stolen" the crystal ball from the publicity apartment that had been set up for an interview and photographs and put it on our mantel at home.

"It says you'll follow me wherever I need you."

"There you are then," she says, and takes a sip of her coffee.

When I first started in pictures over a year ago, she, along with my brother and sister, left Cincinnati—and my father—to be with me in New York City. I needed my family when I came back from the studio, and I also enjoyed taking them to dinner and shows, and walking the streets of the city with them. I couldn't imagine moving to California on my own. So her answer gives me much solace.

I have been in two dozen films in two years. Most of those have been roles in which I've played vengeful, money and sex-seeking women, intent on ruining men. The studio even managed to warp Cleopatra into a greedy, wanton figure. I've tried desperately to play more wholesome characters, a heroine here and there. But it seems I am trapped. I can't convince the public, nor the studio that I am anything but a wicked woman.

I pet Chass, who has settled in my lap. I named him after the famed Egyptologist, Emile Chassinat, whose books I read in my research for *Cleopatra*. He has been a spirited companion on set, creating mischief that amuses me more than it may some others.

Another hour or so and we will reach our next stop; Topeka. Shortly after that, Florence, where I will judge the vamp contest. Those poor girls probably don't even understand what they are emulating.

"What is a vamp anyway?" I say aloud.

"What do you mean?" Mother asks.

"Oh, nothing. Just bother I'm thinking about."

"Because you are always in your own head, Theda. You think too much."

"I know, I should be more grateful to my characters—and I am! I love being an actor. But I also love my fans. And sometimes I feel I am doing them a disservice playing these roles where I besmirch my own gender, when really, I am a *feministe.*"

My mother sets her coffee cup on the table. She moves Chass' tail further around his body onto my lap and slides up against me. She takes my hand and holds it in her fist. "You can be whatever you need to be up there on the screen. It's what you do in the real world that matters. People know this. They like to believe, for an hour and a half, that you are a screen goddess, an Egyptian princess. But when it comes down to it, everyone just wants to know the real Theda Bara. And when they find out, they love you even more for the stark contradiction."

This is why I need my mother.

"Which ones?" Louise asks, holding two different earrings up to each of Miriam's ears.

"The pearl," Lenore answers. She holds Mother's earrings up to her own ears to assess herself in the mirror.

Louise puts the rejected one back into its box and moves

Miriam's hair aside to screw one earring and then the other onto her earlobe.

"Not too tight, Louise!" Miriam says, cringing.

"One last look, Miriam. What do you think?" Lenore turns Miriam around to face the mirror.

Miriam sees how Louise has shaped her thin lips, how the dark liner makes her irises contrast dramatically in the whites of her eyes. Her hair hangs down on one side, a decorative comb of Louise's on the other, her waves draping over her shoulders. For a moment, she pretends to be a stranger to herself. She glimpses a glamorous young woman, maybe even pretty, before her vision retracts, and she sees only herself again underneath the face paint and wonders how anyone could be fooled.

"Look at her!" Louise says. "She is gonna melt the butter on their griddle!"

"And ole' Theda will be so spooked she'll hightail it right back to New York. You just watch, Miriam!"

"You really think so?"

"Absolutely! Lenore, go get some of Mother's magazines so we can remind her how much she looks like her."

Lenore races off to fetch the magazines.

"This is the beginning of the rest of your life," Louise says, patting down the sequins on the shoulders of her dress.

And Miriam lets herself believe this. She basks in Lenore's praise and feels a blossoming under Louise's inspection.

Lenore returns with several copies of their mother's *Photoplay* magazines and splays them out on the bed.

Louise and Lenore adore motion picture magazines and hover over Mother when a new issue arrives. They pore through them, not so much reading the plot lines and directors' notes like Mother does, but analyzing and commenting upon the styles of the actresses and the dashing looks of the men.

Miriam is not as familiar with the magazines. She doesn't much care about fashion, and she doesn't much care for sitting still through motion pictures either. She prefers playing outside, even when the prairie days become cold. She plays field hockey for their school in the spring, and basketball in hated bloomers in the autumn.

Her sisters swish through the magazines until Louise picks one out.

Just then, Mother calls from the downstairs foyer, "We need to leave in twenty minutes if we're going to stop at Great-Aunt May's for her boa."

Louise thrusts the magazine at her, "This one has Theda on the cover."

Her sisters rush out of the room to get ready, leaving Miriam in sudden solitude. There, on the cover of May's *Photoplay*, is Theda in profile. It isn't the 'vamp' Theda she is used to seeing, but a tamer version. She flips through the magazine, bypassing all the advertisements for things like typewriters and correspondence schools. She pauses at a full-page portrait of Mae Murray, "The Girl with the Bee-Stung Lips." Miriam thinks she'd much prefer to be her look-alike.

She finally finds Theda tucked in the middle of the magazine, a two-page collage of photos. Miriam examines them for something she can use. The images look to have been taken in Theda's home. One looks as if the photographer has caught the actress dusting her mantel, another shows her reading, and another writing at a desk. It occurs to Miriam that maybe the actress wants to be seen doing something other than pretending, other than dressing up and making faces for the camera. Still, Theda has that something that makes her an enigma. She has a defiant lift to her chin, an inquisitive tilt that prompts Miriam to wonder who the actress really is, and what she is thinking.

An hour or so later, the train slows. I set down my book and check my hair and makeup in the oval mirror. I watch out the window as the station comes into view. All along the platform, people are gathered. They wave and shout. Some people hold up pictures of me. I see a banner held up among several women: *We Love Our Vamp*. I go to the window and wave back, my heart swelling with gratitude and pride.

As soon as the train stops completely, Chass bolts to his feet and waits at the compartment door. My mother puts aside her embroidery and stands to straighten out her clothes.

"You could stay, if you want to keep out of the sun," I tell her. "This is only a short stop, twenty minutes or so."

"No, I'll come. Chass isn't the only one feeling jiggy."

I take her hat from the ornate hook beside her berth and hand it to her.

Chass yips at the door, commanding it to open, and I bend down to attach his leash.

"Chass, you've been a rotter this trip," I say. "Never sitting still."

"I told you, Border Terriers are a handful. All they want to do is chase and dig, chase and dig," my mother says, as she arranges her hat on her head. "Our neighbors, the Rozens, had one. You're too young to remember, but that little dog did a lot of damage to their fence line. He ran around the neighborhood dropping messes anywhere he desired."

"Alright, Mother. Are you ready?"

The sound of people calling and cheering is amplified by the open doors.

As we exit our compartment, a porter walks up and hands me a folded piece of paper. I know what it is without opening it. It is a wireless from my publicist reminding me of the time and place of the contest at our next stop. It is very important to the studio that I do these publicity stunts, such as judging vamp contests. But what I really love, beyond acting itself, is what waits outside these doors—all those people.

"Thank you," I say to the porter, and he tips his hat and steps aside for us to pass.

As I reach the open door, the clamor outside that sounded so welcoming before, has become disgruntled. That's when I see several porters attempting to herd the throng off the platform and out through the station.

Several people see me as I come into view and resume their cheers and attempts to approach me. In my chest is a warm bubble that threatens to burst. I wave at the crowd and the cheers rise.

Chass has no patience for dramatizing my entrance, and he trots on, again forgetting he is such a tiny thing. Before I can stop him, he tries to alight the train on his own and tumbles onto the platform with a yelp. A mixture of gasps and chuckles issues from the crowd.

I hasten down to scoop him up. "Oh, my eager pet. Come here." I cuddle him to my chest. "I'll keep you safe, I promise."

A reporter holds up his notepad and makes his way toward me.

"Miss Bara! May I interview you?" he shouts. "Miss Bara, please!"

The porter beside me, who assists my mother down, steps toward the reporter with his hand held up. I put a reassuring hand on the porter's arm.

"Certainly, you may interview me."

"Thank you, Miss Bara. Stephen Frain from the Topeka Daily. Now, is this your first time in Topeka? And do you think you'll come again?"

"Well, yes, this is my first time in Topeka. But I won't see much in the fifteen minutes we have, will I? But I do plan to come again. After all, I travel back and forth from the east coast to the west frequently, and I don't see that ending anytime soon. Perhaps one of those times I will be able to spend more time among you lovely folk." The crowd around us explodes.

"Can you tell us about your next picture, Miss Bara?" The reporter has to yell. The crowd quietens down, attempting to hear my response.

"I'm afraid, on this trip, I'm only able to discuss *Cleopatra*, my current picture," I say.

"Do you really believe you are a reincarnation of Cleopatra?"

"How else am I able to embody her feelings? What else would explain my memories of crossing the Nile on barges to Karnak and Luxor as plainly as I recall crossing the Hudson on a ferry?"

This causes the crowd to laugh, and I laugh along with them.

I pick Chass up to hold him in my arms. "Well, I must take this little one to do his private business and for a little run around before we're cooped up again."

"Thank you, Miss Bara. You're so kind. Topeka loves you."

I put a hand to my heart and reach for my mother's arm. The porter clears a way for us, leading us toward the side of the station platform.

A little girl runs up to me with a photo ripped from a magazine. "Please, Miss?" She holds the page and a pen out to me.

I hear requests from all around me now, for pictures, autographs. I put Chass down once again and try, as best I can with him pulling on his leash, to autograph the young girl's picture.

"He's a cute little thing," the girl says when I hand her the pen and picture. Chass winds himself around her legs.

The noise rises up, cheering and blowing kisses.

"Would you like to have some pictures?" I ask the crowd.

There isn't a dissenting voice.

"All right, you write to my Broadway address and tell me you were at the depot at Topeka, and I'll send a picture." I wait for the cheers to die down and then speak my New York address as loud as my voice can project.

I walk unhindered behind the porter, my mother at my side, Chass pulling us forward.

When they reach the gymnasium, Miriam watches as girls mill about—some done up in their best rendition of Theda Bara, others there to support or gawk. There are even a few blonde girls, despite the ad's suggestion. Miriam thinks that even with their light looks, they are decidedly sultry and vamp.

The sight of all these girls hoping to achieve the same thing cows her, but she has her sisters by her side. They practically promised she would win. In her heart of hearts, she knows they can't possibly predict such a thing; anyone has as much chance as another. But she wants to believe her sisters. She imagines watching Miss Bara make her way down the row of girls, imagining her looking almost bored until she comes upon Miriam. She imagines the look on Miss Bara's face when she takes her in and realizes that, yes, *this* is the girl. "What is your name, dear heart?" she will say. Miriam had practiced saying her name in the mirror at home, watching the movements of her lips, in the event that she will be asked.

"Miriam Becker," she will say.

"Miriam Becker, it's like looking in a mirror. I need look no further." And Theda will take her hand, pull her from the row of girls, and lift her arm in victory.

But look at her, Miriam thinks, *that girl with the long string of pearls and the feather in her hair.* The glint in the girl's eyes, the way her shoulders are back and her chest is lifted suggests a self-assurance that Miriam wishes she had. If Miriam wins, like her sisters predict, Miriam will become confident like that too.

"Ladies and girls of the contest, please line up on the risers," an announcer calls through a megaphone. Miriam recognizes him as Mr. Beatty, the dapper, bustling owner of the Mayflower Theatre.

Girls jostle around her, and Miriam feels cast about in the flurry. She ends up on the second row of risers. Louise gives her a nod, which should encourage her, but she is a lone leaf in a cold wind, high up in a tree.

"If you pass the initial round of judging, we will announce your name and you will walk across this space between the podium here and your competition," the announcer continues.

"It is my honor to announce what you must already know. That Ms. Bara will be the final judge. We are lucky to have such a distinguished artist grace our humble city for the short time she is here. But she is a busy lady on her way to work, all the way in Burbank, California!"

There is a gust of applause before the theatre owner speaks again. "Judges will walk the rows now and make their notes while we await Ms. Bara's appearance."

The girls fall silent as the judges walk up and down the row of about twenty-some girls, all dressed in dark clothing of various reveal. The judges browse the girls and look up and down, as if looking at paintings in an art museum. They stand in front of select girls and scratch notes on their paper. It's all a little too serious and Miriam begins to feel self-conscious again, silly even, in her mother's black satin pumps, standing here, doing nothing. She'd rather be judged for catching a fly-ball or making a three-pointer in her basketball game.

People follow at a respectful distance as our porter leads us to the station exit.

"What is your name, sir?" I ask the porter.

"Mr. George Roberts, Miss."

"Thank you for all your assistance, Mr. Roberts. My mother and I appreciate your help."

He tips his hat.

Directly out the doors is a busy road filled with all manner of cars and horse-drawn vehicles. Narrower roads, just as busy, run perpendicular to the station. But just to the left side is a grassy area with a couple of well-maintained trees and several benches.

Some of the crowd tapers off.

"So long, Miss Bara!"

"Thank you, Miss!"

My mother lets go of my arm and sits on the nearest bench.

I let Chass down and unclip his leash. He dashes to a tree and lifts his leg to claim it. He does the same to the next tree, which causes much laughter.

"A couple more minutes, Miss, if you please," our porter says.

"Yes, thank you, Mr. Roberts."

I whistle sharply for Chass to return. I squat down with the leash in my hand as Chass races toward me. He comes at me so fast I lean back on my heels preparing for impact and almost topple back. At the last moment, he swerves and proceeds to sprint around and around, skirting the crowd, loving the attention and laughter.

"Another showman in the family!" my mother says, as she gets up.

"Chass! You rotter!" I laugh. "Come here, Chass, come on."

The porter shifts on his feet and Chass continues to run in circles, his tongue lolling out—such joy, such exuberance.

I squat down again and, as he comes toward me, I reach out for him. Instead of pummeling into me or veering away, he bolts right past.

"Chass!" I immediately follow, trotting after him in my high heels, my long skirt brushing the ground.

I hear the crowd a ways behind me, but I can't pay attention to them.

"Help," I cry to the porter. Chass runs unfettered toward the busy road, intoxicated by his freedom.

The porter passes me, his long legs gaining speed. But Chass continues his blind run, never once looking back. I stop and the crowd stops with me. I cover my face with my hands; I can't bear to look.

And then, a collective gasp from the crowd, the screech of brakes, the scream of a horse and a tumbling crash.

There is a slowly building bustle in the gymnasium, heightened conversation. A man in a boater hat hustles up to the theatre owner watching from the podium. Miriam sees Mr. Beatty's arms collapse to his side. She looks to her mother and sees her knitted eyebrows, which turn smooth again once Miriam catches her eye. Louise, beside Mother, uses her fingers to draw out a smile on her face, reminding Miriam to paint one on her own. As Miriam urges the muscles into place, the judges sense the disturbance and turn away from the contestants to approach the podium.

"We have some unfortunate news, folks," the announcer says. "It is with utmost disappointment that we inform you Miss Bara will not be attending after all."

Miriam thinks he might actually cry—a grown man! Heat rises up in her chest at the thought.

"I appreciate all of you being here, and despite this misfortune, the show must go on! I myself will choose the winner based on the finalists chosen by our panel. May the best vamp win!"

Miriam doesn't hear the last few sentences. All the air has been sucked out of the room, leaving only a rushing sound in her ears. She looks to her mother and sisters. Lenore looks stricken, mirroring everyone's disappointment. Her mother gives her a compassionate smile that is already embracing her. But it is Louise's questioning look, pointed at her, that reminds Miriam to look inside herself. She finds that, though she is keenly disappointed, she is also relieved. Relieved of the possibility of even greater disappointment, and relieved that she will not be judged for her ability to pose as someone who also pretends to be something she's not. Miriam has no doubt that Theda Bara would have recognized this in her. Because she saw something in Theda in those magazine photos that she couldn't put into words. She saw in Theda a woman who wanted to be seen for who she was.

Miriam lifts her chin and steps down from the riser. Lenore and Louise watch her approach with marvel at the sudden conviction their sister seems to possess. She reaches her family, and her sisters put their arms about her.

"Let's go," she tells them.

Together, they leave behind the vamped up girls and make their way through the still muttering, collectively disappointed crowd, and out the doors.

AMBITION'S WAKE

By Anne Johnston

ARI'S EYES TRACED THE lazy patterns of dust motes floating through the amber-toned lamplight of the modest office. The baritone chatter of her colleague melded with the comforting hum of vehicles passing by on the rainy streets below, lulling her into a comfortable fog.

"Isn't that right, Ari?"

The words lingered in her daze but failed to pull her back to the moment. She gave a noncommital nod.

Jonathan cleared his throat sharply. His clearly formed wish for her attention felt like a sudden jerk on the end of a leash. She kept her eyelids soft as her gaze settled on his face—all severe angles and annoyance. He knew as well as she that his wish bound her to do his bidding, but she need not grant it with eagerness. She glanced slowly from Jonathan to the man sitting across the desk in front of him.

He shook his head in exasperation and leaned back in his perfectly worn leather chair. "I was just telling Mr. Smith here that locating people is a specialty of ours. Isn't that right?"

"In a way," she said. Jonathan's eyes narrowed but refused to meet hers, looking instead at the potential client. "Assuming the person you are looking for is related to you in some way, then, yes, we are undoubtedly the best in the world."

At her pronouncement, the little man sitting in front of Jonathan began twisting a handkerchief in his hands and bouncing his knee, dislodging his fedora. As he fumbled to reclaim the hat from the floor, he mumbled, "But the rumors—"

"Are just that, dear," Ari said. She sat back in her chair and turned her attention to the patter of raindrops on the window behind Jonathan. He hadn't released his wish yet, so she was compelled to continue listening as he expertly soothed the client and bade him continue with his thought.

"You found Gable and Lewis's kid. That's what people say anyway. When she was hidden in that orphanage." Mr. Smith looked back and forth between Jonathan and Ari for reassurance. Finding none in their blank expressions, he pressed on. "You found her and confirmed she was Clark's daughter, no matter what her mother insisted. That *was* you?"

"We can't comment on that." Jonathan shifted uneasily in his seat.

Ari's lips twitched up at one corner and she looked at him sidelong, but remained silent.

The little man stopped fidgeting, emboldened rather than deterred by the denial. "And your role in the Wineville Chicken Coop case?"

Jonathan let out a laugh that had almost become unfamiliar to Ari, it had been so long since she'd last heard it. She softened slightly as the deep, honey sound conjured up her memories of him as a younger man.

"That was quite a while ago," she said. "One of our first cases."

"You uncovered it by tracking down that Walter Collins kid, right?"

She nodded. "As I said, finding family members is a unique strength of…" she paused, looking at Jonathan and weighing her words for a moment, "…ours."

The abdication of credit chafed her, wiping away the moment of nostalgia. She frowned as she watched concern settle again into the creases of the man's face.

"It's not a family member you are looking for, dear?"

Mr. Smith shook his head slightly. He looked down at the twisted handkerchief in his lap.

"But you find kids," he said through gritted teeth.

"You think this kid is in trouble?" Ari leaned in, her pulse quickening a beat, and all pretense of disinterest melting away.

He dropped the handkerchief and leaned back in his chair. Staring at the ceiling, he let out a long, loud breath and shook his head.

"Nothing like that," he said. "I just need to know whether the kid actually exists. There is a rumor about an illegitimate child belonging to a state legislator. I need you to confirm it for me."

"Ah," said Jonathan. "I take it you are here on behalf of his political opponent?"

"No."

"You work for the legislator, then?"

"Not yet." The man sat straighter in the chair, pulling back his shoulders, and looked Jonathan square in the eye. "Assuming you can do your job, I will be able to secure my own."

Jonathan nodded. "Well, you know our rates, Mr. Smith, and clearly you have heard about our success. We can certainly take on a conventional investigation into this matter for you.

"All right then." The client reached into his jacket pocket and produced a thick envelope. "In the meantime, here's what I have to get you started."

The two men stood as Jonathan took the envelope and glanced inside it briefly. They shook hands and exchanged some final pleasantries before Mr. Smith shrugged into his raincoat, donned his fedora, and headed out into the night. With the client gone, Jonathan's wish was fulfilled. Ari could go back to ignoring him as he pocketed the money from the envelope and laid the sparse array of documents out on the desk.

Ari's thoughts slipped back to the cases Mr. Smith had mentioned. Those were the sort of investigations that made her excited to work with Jonathan. After eons of being attached to men who used her powers as a djinn to dominate and control others, Jonathan's earnestness was an endearing change of pace. She fondly recalled the bright-eyed man as he was on the day he'd returned from The Great War. His grandfather had not predicted just how much Jonathan's time away impacted him. If he'd known, the old warhorse might have had second thoughts about gifting the lamp to the young man.

While the horror of combat had clearly touched Jonathon, leaving him with nightmares and a slight limp, it also emboldened him with a quiet determination to serve and protect. Unfortunately, his injuries kept him out of the police force, and he'd shown no aptitude for medical or charity work. His wishes during that period were sporadic and ill-formed. He hadn't known what he wanted, much less how to articulate those desires. His family, and the Lampkeeper Organization to which they belonged, hadn't helped matters either. To this day, they pressured Jonathan to use her powers to elevate himself and others within the group to prominence.

Initially, his wishes focused on strengthening the familial bonds of his old platoon buddies. Erratic and sweet, he'd made wishes that benefited the people in his life in surprisingly ordinary ways. He talked incessantly in those days about the dignity of simple people doing simple things well and with passion. It warmed Ari's heart.

Eventually, Jonathan expanded this philosophy beyond his immediate circle of acquaintances. Ari's natural ability to grant wishes regarding familial ties buoyed his desire to help the little guy by seeking out and correcting misdeeds. Cheating spouses, missing children, long lost relatives, misplaced family heirlooms—these had become the tasks to which they turned their attention, much to the chagrin of the Lampkeepers. Instead of being used to arrange prosperous marriages or forced into procreating half djinn children for the good of the organization,

Ari had delighted in raining down deserved punishment for infidelity and found fulfillment in reuniting families. It felt, for a time, like returning to the era before Solomon, when she'd been closer to a goddess than a slave.

Those feelings changed, however, as most did over time. Although Jonathan allowed her more personal freedom than previous Lampkeepers, in the end, she was no less owned by him than she had been by his grandfather. This was made increasingly clear to her as their cases became more pedestrian. Jonathan grew frustrated with her obvious boredom. His wishes for her involvement were ever more constrained, focused on clearly defined tasks and specific outcomes rather than allowing her to use her judgment and creativity.

Ari heard Jonathan talking to himself about the new job. A stream of conscious babble about stakeout locations and what he needed to prepare interrupted her solitary reminiscing. She roused and crossed the room to the coat rack.

Gathering her belongings, she said over her shoulder, "Give my best to Judith and the kids, dear."

"Fine, but be at the corner of Baker and Aurora tomorrow at eleven. Bring lunch, would you?"

The next morning, as she prepared their lunch, Ari's hand suddenly stilled as she poured coffee into the thermos. She watched the stream of fragrant liquid thin to a slow drip. She blinked in time with the lingering drops and wrinkled her nose. She'd prepared the lunch as requested, almost out of habit, but it hadn't been an actual wish.

When he'd met and married Judith, Ari assumed she would become the live-in help, just as she had with many of her prior Lampkeepers. But Jonathan opted not to inform his wife about Ari's true nature. Instead, he slowly restricted all non-business-related interactions between them. As his children grew, even the usual office lunches gave way to extra family time—in which she was not included. Ari frowned down at the neatly packed boxes of sandwiches and sliced fruit as she added the thermos.

When the foodstuffs provided no additional insight, she gave a little snort and slammed the percolator back on the stove. Ari closed her eyes and called to mind a crystal clear image of Jonathan. Standing next to him, she conjured up her most recent memory of Judith's likeness. Between them, she could make out the strand of knotted connections that bound them in marriage. Despite her repeated explanations that her magic could not actually make a person fall in love with another, Jonathan had insisted that she not provide any type of blessing or interference in their union. He wanted to be certain their relationship was "real." As though her magic were fictional. She snorted again and focused on the bonds of Jonathan's marriage.

Though every marriage started with a single strong core, time and shared experiences added new strands that wove into and knotted around that center. In a good pairing, the new strands and knots strengthened the original bond and thickened the tie.

Between Jonathan and Judith, Ari could see definite fraying. She sighed sadly and opened her eyes. She folded the cloth closed over the lunches, tying the corners into a bundle. Settling the luncheon into a tote with a book and her wallet, Ari wrapped her scarf about her head and neck and picked up her sunglasses. With a glance at the clock ticking away on the mantel, she hustled out to catch the streetcar.

The day was bright, and a slight breeze off the bay managed to beat back the smog more than usual. Ari could even make out the top of the new City Hall tower as she approached the designated meeting place. Yet shadows lingered in her mind.

As she approached Jonathan's car, Ari could not shake her newfound insights about the state of the man's marriage. His clear wish for her to remain out of it chafed against her very nature, but she was as bound by that wish as he was bound by his vows. She took a slow, deep breath to steel herself. With one swift tug, she opened the passenger door and slipped into the seat.

The tension of a troubled home clearly followed Jonathan to the stakeout. He was writing on a notepad propped against the steering wheel. The awkwardness of the position was heightened by the visible tension in his shoulders, which hunched forward as he scribbled angrily. Ari settled her bag on the bench seat between them and leaned back, feigning indifference as she looked blankly out the large expanse of windshield.

Jonathan ignored her entirely. He dropped the notebook into his lap and snatched a pair of binoculars off the dashboard. If the legislator in question were close by, it would be simple enough for her to determine the number and nature of his familial ties. She watched the slight sway of fabric in the breeze where it had come loose from the car ceiling and waited for Jonathan's wish to direct her.

Jonathan continued to ignore her presence, swapping the binoculars for the notepad. Ari squinted, appraising him critically.

"I brought ham salad," she said. "I hope that's okay, dear."

She knew it was. It was his favorite, in fact. Yet, his only reply was a subtle, one-shoulder shrug. Her face puckered at his obstinate refusal to engage. She dug around in the tote to retrieve her book.

"Fine. Just let me know when the legislator arrives, will you?"

"He's in the café down the street."

She gaped at him as he dropped the notepad and grabbed the thermos of coffee from the tote, avoiding her eyes. He poured a cup of coffee, replaced the thermos, and returned to the binoculars.

"Well?" Ari asked.

"Still in there, far as I can tell."

"So?"

His eyes met hers for the first time since she'd gotten into the vehicle nearly an hour before. They narrowed in challenge. "So what?"

"So why haven't you sent me in there? I can go place an order for carryout and have the family connections back to you in fifteen minutes."

"No, you can't!" Jonathan roared. She reflexively recoiled, pressing against the door. He huffed, shook his head a few times, and returned to watching the café through the binoculars.

With a tentative hand, Ari touched his shoulder and lowered her voice as she asked, "Is everything all right, dear?"

At her touch, some of the tension released and his shoulders sagged. Jonathan's stony expression melted into a frown, and his eyes softened as he dropped his hands to his lap. With a sigh that wrenched Ari's heart, he said, "You already know it isn't. You've been so smug about it the last few weeks, too. Don't start pretending on me now, doll."

He shrugged her hand from his shoulder and returned to his notepad.

"I didn't actually," she whispered. His pencil stopped scratching. He shot her a sidelong glance, followed by a raised eyebrow. "At least not until this morning." Waving at the mostly still packed lunch, she said, "It's the first time in—what?—ten years that you've asked me to make anything more than a rum and coke."

He gave her a lopsided attempt at a smile. "I suppose that was a giveaway, huh?"

Ari shrugged and glanced up at the café. "What does any of that have to do with not wanting me to close this case for you, quick and easy?"

Jonathan shook his head. "Nothing, I suppose." He refused to meet her eyes again, instead fiddling with the pencil and notepad in his lap.

"Yet, there's still no wish," Ari said. "You know I can't use magic for much without you actually wanting me to."

"But I don't really want you to, do I? I want to know I can do these things on my own. But the reality is that I can't, can I? I'll never know if I could have made a real living as PI without my family, you, and the Lampkeepers." His lip curled slightly on the last word.

"And Roosevelt wonders if he'd ever have become President without his family connections. So what? We've had this same conversation a number of times before, dear. We've always worked through it. What makes this time different? And what on God's green Earth does it have to do with your marriage? I've stayed out of it."

"I know." After a few beats, Jonathan lowered his eyes from the ceiling and shifted slightly in the seat to face her more fully. "It's Arthur." Ari's eyebrows shot up at the mention of his son. Concern settled into dark crevices of her face, but she said nothing, allowing him to gather his thoughts.

"He's fourteen now." Jonathan rubbed his forehead. "He starts high school in the fall. The Lampkeepers want him to attend one of their institutions. Be trained for leadership." He sighed heavily. "Learn all the family secrets."

"You haven't told him anything?"

"Not even about you. That's why you haven't been around the family much. Honestly, I would have just given you your lamp and set you free years ago if the organization hadn't threatened us. Knowing we have one of the few original djinn of Solomon attached to the family is the only thing that's kept them from trying anything."

"And why doesn't that knowledge stop them from getting

Arthur into their school?" she asked.

"They sent a welcome packet to Judith," he said. "Nothing that says it's about genies and magic, just a lot of slick pamphlets about the quality of education and the prestigious nature of the scholarship Arthur's supposed to have won. I can't tell her why I don't want him going there without revealing everything. Best case scenario, she thinks I'm crazy. Worst case, she believes me and realizes how much of my life is a lie."

"It is not." Ari tried to pat his hand, but he pulled away.

"In any case, right now Judith thinks I'm sacrificing our son to some Communist ideal of the everyman because I want to send him to the local school instead."

They sat in silence for some time before Ari opted to unpack the food. Busying herself with the menial tasks of caretaking relaxed her body and mind. Jonathan robotically took the items handed to him and began to eat, all the while gazing out the windshield at the café.

He stopped with the sandwich halfway to his mouth. "I know it isn't fair to you," he said, defeat warring with stoicism in his timbre. "But I don't want to wish for you to solve this case. That's the easy way."

This was a familiar line of discourse between them. Ari said, "You know that's not true. You have never used my powers to pursue the path of least resistance. The easy way out would be to wish that the Lampkeepers could never interfere with you or your family. Or to give in to them and make the types of wishes they want. You have always given real thought to your desires and forged your own path."

Though she didn't say so, she suspected most of the wishes he made were more for her benefit than his own—little things to ease the inevitable pressure of magical buildup within her.

"You are strong. You can afford to forge your own path, in part, because of what the Lampkeepers gave you."

He momentarily broke her gaze. "Yeah… you."

"Education, experience, and a network of value," she said, more kindly than before. "My presence alone would have meant nothing without that, dear. You must realize how much more prepared for the realities of the world you were than most people, even before you received my lamp."

Jonathan's eyes darted to the café. "Let's get on with it then," he said. "You good with doing it on the move? He just left the restaurant. We can tail him to the end of block without raising any alarms, but that'll be all you get for now."

She shook her head. "You know all I need is your wish… and maybe the binoculars, dear. There's no need to be so dramatic about it all."

He gave a lopsided grin and winked at her. "Maybe I like the drama, doll."

She took the binoculars and felt the clarity of his wish take shape around her.

"Tell me what you see about his family."

As he vocalized the desire, she homed in on the man on the sidewalk. The words gave the wish a solidity that drove her magic toward the target. She focused on shaping the wish so that, as the magic made contact with the legislator, her world exploded into a visible web of connections emanating from the man.

"He comes from a large family, does he?"

"Yeah, five brothers and two sisters. Lord only knows how many nieces and nephews."

"Nine to date," she said. "And four children. Though one of the threads is cut short."

"Makes sense. He and his wife had three kids. The youngest died in the crib at four months." At that revelation, Ari's heart sank. The loss of a child was always hard, and being able to see the impact made her uneasy. Where the thread connected to his marriage bond, the rope had blackened and begun to rot. The damage was extensive but not yet fatal. Thin new strands of connection overlaid the old and suggested healing amidst the pain.

"The fourth child. Older or younger than the others?" Jonathan's voice pulled her away from the sight of the wounded marriage.

"Younger."

"Any ideas on the mother?"

Ari dropped the binoculars to her lap. The world, uncomplicated by visual networks, snapped back into focus around her. She rubbed her eyes and said, "In the café. A waitress, I'd hazard. And there's some item, a family heirloom, which connects all the children and their father—something like a dress."

Jonathan nodded and jotted the information on his notepad. He flipped it shut with one hand and quickly shoved the remains of their lunch aside, before starting the car and pulling into traffic.

"We aren't going to talk to the woman, dear?" Ari asked.

"No need. I have a pretty good idea who she is and what the heirloom is. And that's the piece that matters," he said, with a sparkle in his eye. He refused to share his hunch, grinning with the secret all the way to steps of the church.

Jonathan managed to tone down his excitement as he inquired about christening records. Left alone in the cathedral, Ari contemplated her Lampkeeper. It occurred to her that he hadn't actually needed to use her powers, but had done so only to confirm what he already suspected. She bowed her head in silent prayer, recalling the Divine directive to all djinn to serve mankind with their magic. With the eyes of Jude looking down on her, she wondered whether her service to Jonathan was valuable any longer. It clearly caused him significant anxiety, and she did not know what the benefits truly were—beyond keeping the more sadistic elements of the Lampkeeper organization at bay.

Before the musings could settle into a full-blown existential crisis, Jonathan returned with a triumphant grin and a folder tucked under his arm.

"Back to the office to make a few calls," he said, extending his arm to escort Ari from the church. "Then, I expect we'll be heading to meet the legislator with our Mr. Smith quite soon".

Quite soon turned out to be the following day at teatime. The pair met Mr. Smith outside a large house in the Echo Park area. The men shook hands and exchanged greetings, then the door was opened and the trio were escorted to a sitting room. The well-appointed chamber had a library of law books and a modest secretarial desk along the far wall. Tucked among the books on the shelves and the papers stacked neatly on the desk were photographs of smiling children. A framed child's drawing hung beside the man's diplomas, and a handful of stray toys had been lost to the recesses of one corner under the desk.

Ari smiled at the sight. Although a typical professional veneer marked the space, it was touched deeply by family. She suspected the same could be said of the man that occupied one of the chairs in the middle of the room.

He rose to greet them with warmth and only a slight undercurrent of concern. "Please come in. Come in and take a seat. We'll have tea brought in momentarily. Or would you lot prefer coffee?"

Ari smiled again as the man kissed her hand formally and escorted her to the nearest chair. She momentarily forgot the purpose of the visit.

But Mr. Smith was not so beguiled. "Thank you, Senator," he said, as he settled into a chair and dropped the folder on the coffee table between them. "Tea would be fine. What we have to discuss is quite delicate, as you may have already suspected."

The legislator looked at the folder and then at Mr. Smith. He nodded slightly and moved to sit directly across from the man.

"No matter what it is you think you've found," he said bluntly, "first realize that my votes are not for sale. If that is understood, then we can continue this business. Otherwise, I'll ask you to show yourselves out."

Mr. Smith inclined his head in agreement. The legislator settled back into his seat and gestured for him to continue. Jonathan and Mr. Smith presented their evidence of the man's infidelity. The final piece of the story, about the resulting child, came as a light tap announced the arrival of the tea tray.

"This is quite a story," the man said, as they took a moment to pour their drinks. "No real proof, however."

Mr. Smith slid a photo from the folder. Ari caught the barest glimpse of a beaming woman holding her child in his beautifully unique christening gown. The same gown was clearly displayed in other pictures within the room. As the picture was passed to the legislator, the woman serving their tea stiffened. The men did not appear to notice, but the motion drew Ari's attention.

The woman, whom Ari had taken for a servant, was dressed simply but with immaculate attention to detail. Ari watched her retreat from the room. She excused herself and followed. Ari could see now that this woman was clearly the man's wife, yet Ari could sense no serious upset in her cool demeanor.

Ari stopped in the powder room just before the kitchen. When she emerged, she found the wife still standing in the kitchen, where she leaned against the counter and looked down the hallway toward the sitting room. One arm was crossed over, cupping the elbow of the other, which held a cup of strong coffee. The aroma floated delicately on the air.

Though she didn't really care for the drink herself, Ari approached the woman and asked, "Would you mind if I join you for a cup in here?"

The woman gave her a smirk and a half shrug. She set her mug on the counter and poured another for Ari.

"The cream and sugar are on the tray in the sitting room, but you could get a bit of milk from the jug in the fridge if you like." She handed over the cup and resumed her original pose.

"That's fine. Thank you, dear." Ari settled into a similar position beside her. The women stood watching the men talk. There was a fair bit of nodding now; they seemed to be reaching an agreement of sorts.

"So, what is it that your Mr. Smith wants exactly?"

"He's not my anything, but I believe he wants a job."

The woman laughed, surprising Ari. "Ambitious, then. He'll fit right in." She turned to the sink and set the mug into it, then gripped the edge of the counter and looked out the window. "I suppose it could have been worse."

"This must be quite hard on you. Infidelity is always hard on a marriage, but an illegitimate child just makes it—"

The woman waved off Ari's words. "I always knew about it—or at least strongly suspected. I don't care, but the press would. The voters. This information could have come out in a much more damaging way." She turned back to look at her husband.

Ari's mouth hung open as she registered the affection still present in the woman's gaze. There was no hint of malice or disappointment. "But he was unfaithful to you."

"I never really expected him to be faithful. That was a promise he made many years ago. I've never put much faith in promises—much too easily broken," the woman said, before returning her attention to the men. "I would rather trust in his ambition."

The woman raised her chin a bit as she continued, "That man has plans for this world, and he is going places in it. As his wife, I will go there with him. All the rest is just…" Her lip curled slightly. "…empty promises."

Ari looked down the hall at the men. As a djinn, she could actually sense the scope of their varying desires. The legislator had big wants and wishes, and he had the drive to make them happen—with or without magic. Mr. Smith similarly emanated a sense of urgent dedication, though his intentions were less clear to Ari. In contrast, Ari's gaze settled on Jonathan. His ambitions had cooled. They were small and tightly constrained, like the limited wishes he'd made in recent years. Ari frowned as she considered the woman's words.

The men concluded their business with a round of handshakes, and Ari hurried down the hall to Jonathan's side. As the pair settled into the car, Ari thought about her likely future attached to a man of such little ambition. She needed someone to own her lamp and make wishes, and Jonathan was a safer pairing than many of her prior Lampkeepers. At the thought of those owners, she cringed and tried to remind herself of the dignity of simple tasks done well.

Yet the question of her future lingered. As both the horizon and her spirits darkened, she fell into the sliver of sunset amid the clouds and took a chance.

"Jonathan, out of curiosity, what does Arthur want to do when he grows up?"

THE SEA PROVIDES

By Thomas Brown

THE SEA HAD ALWAYS provided a good life.

Donald looked out the window, watching a bolt of lightning strike from the heavens to terminate in the roiling black seas. The blue water of the day turned into a dense black moving mass at night with as much life as anything else. The day had begun with clear skies that turned into showers as the sea pulled more and more water from the sky to replenish itself. By evening, the distant sound of thunder had shaken the Flanagan Isles as the waves crashed ashore. The island stood in the sea alone, poking at the eye of God Himself.

Occasionally, He did His best to wipe what angered Him away. The growing waves were crashing against the outcropping of granite that was offensive to God's eye, and the growing waves were his wrath. The storm's powerful winds shook the building, and being one hundred and fifty feet away from the black of the ocean swells served little comfort.

The Occasional Lighthouse Keeper, a title held by two men

who rotated to fill out the three-man crew, was responsible for the lantern itself. The other two, the permanent Lighthouse Keepers, maintained the rest of the buildings, though to be honest, everyone did a bit of everything.

Donald had tried to describe the storms and how they related to his job to his two boys, but the words escaped him. His lack of education defeated the indelible images imprinted in his mind. But one word always came to mind. Anger. More of a discussion of God. God's charity, his love, and again his wrath. It was God doing battle with the creations of man.

At least, that was the story he told his boys.

The Permanent Keepers, Thomas and James, had left a short while before, their oilskins wrapped around them as protection from both wind and wave. It was their job to check the provision boxes for the landing area. They'd heard the rending of metal in the lighthouse, even as the storm raged around them. Both men had left him alone in his perch high above the sea, as the winds howled around him like an Irish banshee.

The banshee was the first thing that came to mind. She howled again and again, shrill and long, with only a few seconds' pause to catch her breath.

But it was neither banshee nor wind, but a whistle. A cry for help in the storm. There was a pause, a man catching his breath to empty his lungs of life in the hope for aid.

The sea had always provided a good life.

The thought was the armor with which he wrapped his mind to give himself comfort.

He ignored his oilskins and ran out into the maelstrom, finding the trail down, but only guessing where Thomas and James might be.

The shrill sound cut through the storm again. This time it was stronger; somewhere in front of him, maybe. Donald held onto the guide rope, slick with rain and sea water, and let it take him to his destination.

A bolt of lightning split the darkness of the night asunder, lighting up a man grasping the guideline, keeled over its edge like a landlubber in his first pitched sea. The light faded, the thunder shaking the very land he tried so hard to keep his feet on.

He made his way to the man as another blast from his whistle, clear now, left him as he lay pitched over the line, staring over its edge at the sea. Donald could no longer feel his hand as he grabbed the man by the shoulder.

He pulled the man back and realized it was Thomas.

His face was filled with fear, a soul-searing fear. His whistle had fallen from his mouth, but his lips were still pursed in his call for help.

"Where is James?" Donald asked. "How did he go over the edge? Is that why you were there?" Donald had to yell over the wind and the rain. "Where is James?"

"She took him, she took him away," Thomas repeated. His head shook. What he had seen, what had occurred, was beyond what he could comprehend, far beyond any frame of reference his life might hold.

Donald shook the man hard, watching him crumble before

him like a house of cards.

Who took him?

He looked down the path to the sea and out on the night. The storm was advancing on them like a brigade in battle; the night was blacker than any he had ever seen. Then the bolt of lightning illuminated his world, and he realized what he saw wasn't the night at all.

It stood over fifty feet higher than where he stood.

The sea had always provided a good life.

The thought flashed only briefly. But as the thunder rolled over the isle seconds later, always in a losing race against the lightning, it found only emptiness and the vast sea before it.

THE HAND
By Tom MacMahon

MARY ELLEN

TODAY WAS THE DAY. Mary Ellen Emslie, after three long months, was finally going to visit her fiancé in the sanatorium. She was filled with that utter joy of loving the most wonderful man, George Raven. They had met in the office of the radio production factory six months earlier. She had known right away—he was the one for her. He was tall, neatly dressed, straight-backed with a smile that exploded her heart. Sadly, he contracted consumption shortly after they met and was sent to recover in a sanatorium isolated up in the north lakes. It meant a long train ride, but she was prepared. She had her favourite book to read, and daydreaming would fill in the rest.

Mary Ellen danced a little twirl around her room admiring her engagement ring with its beautifully clear, colourless diamond in a silver floral setting. They had bought it together and, although it cost George two months' salary, he hadn't even flinched when she'd picked it out. She loved that about him, his total dedication to her happiness. Until she'd met George and fallen in love, she hadn't understood the magic of those feelings.

Mary Ellen snuggled into her seat for the four-hour train ride. The faint scents of polished leather, cigarette smoke and ladies' perfume formed a pleasing bouquet. She could hardly sit still and finally opened her book to calm her nerves. The train ride seemed interminable until the conductor walked down the aisle announcing her stop. Once off the train, she hailed a cab and was soon on her way.

Her cab stopped in front of the imposing medical establishment. The building reminded her of the Palace of Versaille, which she had read about in a magazine. Long and low with high windows framed by ornate fixtures, it seemed almost a fairy tale castle which held her prince.

"Do you want me to wait, Miss?" said the cabbie.

Mary Ellen answered, " If you don't really mind? They don't allow long visits." She gave him a nice tip for obliging her.

Standing in front of the grand entrance, she looked up and read the inscription over the door. *Spes autem, quae in medicina, invenit.* With the help of her high school Latin, she was able to translate. *Hope is what is found in medicine.*

She laughed at having so much hope for the future and her happiness.

Mary Ellen pushed open the heavy oak doors.

LUKE

Luke Klein gripped the heavy 4' X 8' plasterboard sheet and hauled it out of his truck. He stared up at the dilapidated old Emslie house with its unpainted sidings, sagging gutters and broken windows. It was always his luck to get the worst assignments.

He muttered, "If I didn't have bad luck, I wouldn't have any luck at all."

Even though it was a cold, gray November morning, he sweated with the exertion of moving the seventy-pound sheetrock from his truck onto a pile. He cursed and swore with the aches and pains of the heavy work. Normally, he would have used the roll lifter, but his co-worker had beaten him to it. As usual, he'd been late, and his boss had given him hell for his habitual tardiness. Luke didn't care if he got fired. He just wanted to finish the job and get back home where he could crack open a few beers, turn on the TV and lay back to enjoy his solitude.

Luke, a tall, thin thirty-something Midwesterner, felt no desire to move ahead in the world. He knew the reason wasn't that he was stupid or anything like that. He was just unmotivated. He had no plans for the immediate future and didn't even enjoy the company of his so-called friends. They wanted to get away to bigger and better prospects. As he slid the gyprock sheets up into the house on the plywood ramp he had slapped together, he scowled at the unfairness of it all. He could have won a basketball scholarship to the U, but again, he couldn't muster the enthusiasm to compete for it. Life's demands seemed to require more effort than he could generate.

Now, here he was, standing in the Emslie house foyer attempting to finish off the renovation of the third floor room. It was going to be a long, long haul with the heavy wallboard up three flights of newly polished antique stairway. He had laid down plenty of tarp to prevent scratching, but he was sure, with his luck, something bad was going to happen.

MARY ELLEN

Approaching the long, polished mahogany reception desk, Mary Ellen asked for George Raven and gave the woman at the desk her name.

"Please take a seat and someone will come for you." But as Mary Ellen sat down on the church-like waiting bench, the receptionist added, "If you would rather wait outside in our back garden, I can have the nurse meet you out there?"

It being such a glorious late summer day, Mary Ellen immediately followed the receptionist out the back door.

Mary Ellen strolled around the lush gardens waiting for a nurse to escort her to see George. They were designed in the Greek style complete with alabaster statues, marble plinths and faux ruins scattered about the grounds. The lawns were meticulously groomed and stretched down to the lakeside. Out on the lake, she could just make out a small boat lazily sailing over the placid dark waters. There were two people in the boat, and they seemed to be enjoying each other's company.

Mary Ellen looked away from the scene as a nurse approached her.

"Hello, Miss Emslie. We are still looking for Mr. Raven, shouldn't be too long."

Mary Ellen thanked her, telling her she would be down by the lake waiting for news. The nurse left, and Mary Ellen squinted at the occupants of the small boat as it headed for shore. The once sunny afternoon had suddenly grown overcast. The shadows of menacing clouds moved swiftly over the green lawns, turning them into patches of festering black carpet, but a growing apprehension drew her to the lake. She hurried under a large weeping willow for protection from the coming rain. Her eyesight was poor, so she reached into her purse for her glasses. The little boat was hastening onto shore, and she could now see the passengers.

One was a young girl, another patient she guessed, with her hair and dress messed up as if she had been in a wrestling match. The other was George Raven, who looked much paler and thinner than when they had last seen each other. He, too, was disheveled, but smiling wickedly at the girl. Neither noticed Mary Ellen, who stood in the shade.

George grabbed the girl around her slim waist and tried for a kiss. The girl giggled and said, "George, you are insatiable. Let's wait 'til tonight when everything is quiet and people cannot spy on us!"

George laughed and replied cavalierly, "Okay, Miss Liberties, I plan on taking full advantage of your offer this evening!"

It was then that the girl noticed Mary Ellen standing in the shade and blushed.

George almost fell out of the boat when he saw her, just barely catching himself. He looked at her with a mixture of surprise and anger.

"Jesus Christ, Mary Ellen!" he said. "Where did you come from?"

Mary Ellen didn't reply. She had seen enough. All her hopes and dreams dissolved in the acid of her shock. Her mouth felt dry. She could not catch her breath. Crying, she raced up the lawn toward the garden entrance. Just then, the storm broke and a downpour of cold, biting rain soaked the grounds. George ran after her, wheezing and coughing. He tried to yell, but only rasped, "Stop! I can explain!"

Mary Ellen slipped in the mud and tumbled. She heard George's soggy feet approaching like the paws of a rabid dog, advancing on her, and she scrambled back up and limped toward the building entrance. She was soaked, her dress was in shambles and her ankle ached from the fall. She did not turn, as George, despite his affliction, was still gaining on her. She slipped again, and his wet hand reached out and found the hem of her dress. She desperately tried to pull away as he clawed his way closer.

"Let me go!" she cried. As he finally stood over her, there was a twisted smile on his sodden face.

As George bent to grab her, two burly attendants appeared at the door asking, "Is there a problem here Ma'am?"

Startled, George released her dress, and Mary Ellen scrambled away, pointing and shouting, "There's your problem! Arrest him!"

The two attendants moved toward George, who struggled to get by them. They held him back while he shouted, "Arrest me? What for? Having a little fun? At least I had more fun with her than I'd ever had with you!"

Sobbing, Mary Ellen ran through the building, past the reception area and out the front door. Her driver was enjoying a cigarette near his cab. With her wet dress plastered to her skin, she cried, "Please, please take me back to the station!"

The driver stubbed out his cigarette and quickly opened the door for her. Once inside, he turned to her and asked, "Are you okay, Miss?

Mary Ellen's whole body shivered. She could no longer speak.

LUKE

Luke stopped to take a breather. He had the rest of the day of drywalling to do, including plastering the seams and screw holes. He actually did not mind the mounting of the drywall as much as the effort of bringing it up and into the house. He had been doing this for five years and was quite adept at manipulating sheetrock into place. What he hated most was plastering, with its greasy feel and slimy mess which, of course, he would have to clean up when he was dog tired.

Luke walked over to the dirt-caked window of the old mansion and looked out. When he was a kid, he and his buddies would wait until dark and throw mud and rotten apples from the nearby orchard at the creepy old lady who lived here. She was long gone now, but he recalled how everyone thought she was a witch. She even had a scraggly, old black cat. If she appeared at the upper window, they would yell with fright and scamper away like mice caught out in a moonlit field by a circling hawk. On one occasion, she had flung open the window, scaring the boys into hysterical shrieks when she had leaned out, waving her stump of an arm, sobbing, “Once, I was happy!” As they scattered, they called her names, laughing from relief all the way to safety.

Luke remembered feeling a tiny bit of sorrow as the woman’s distant sobs scratched at his conscience. Now, he just chuckled at the memories.

MARY ELLEN

Mary Ellen lay on her bed, weeping as the last fleeting glow of the day came to an end. The thunderstorm at the sanatorium had followed her home. The night crawled with the deepest black. Thunder and lightning galloped across the sky with unchecked fury. George Raven appeared out of the storm like an unearthly spectre, begging to see her. His clothes were tangled and hung loosely on his bony frame. He was soaked and coughing violently. Mary Ellen’s mother refused to let him in, so he staggered around to her bedroom window.

"Mary Ellen!" he shouted. "You're mine! You need to talk to me!"

She threw the window open and stared in contempt at the figure of a man she had once treasured. She screamed, "Go away! I cannot stand the sight of you!"

He swore and raised his fist at her. "Damn it, Mary Ellen. At least give me the ring so I can get back some of the money I spent on you!"

Aghast at his callousness, Mary Ellen tried to remove the engagement ring, so she could throw it at him, but it wouldn't come off. She tugged and tugged.

George grinned maliciously and said, "See, you can't even get your ring off. That means you will always belong to me."

She spat at him and rushed down to the kitchen. Frantic, she greased up her finger with lard, but still the ring refused to budge. She threw open the door to the cellar. A rush of cold air caressed her from the dark, damp space below. Down in the cellar, she searched for something, anything to remove that dreadful ring. The pliers didn't work. Neither did the vise. Suddenly, she stopped crying as a crazed look of understanding slithered across her face. She looked up at the cellar ceiling as if in prayer.

LUKE

Luke hoisted the last wallboard onto the studs and began to screw it into place. Just as he finished, he felt a rush of cold air, as if a window had been opened. He set down the screwdriver and walked out of the room to look around. All the windows and doors were firmly closed. Luke shook his head and returned to the upper room.

He was hoisting the final panel into place when he heard a sound that jolted him—a loud thump, as if something had been slammed down with an incredible amount of violence. The entire house trembled with the dying echo of the monstrous noise. Luke felt the frantic beating of his heart in his chest, but he convinced himself it was only the house settling. He took in a deep breath and thought of those cold beers awaiting him in his fridge. He kept working.

He was screwing the last fastener into place when he heard another sound. This time a low, cat-like growl floated hungrily out of the darkness to lightly lick at his ears. The growl had a real physical presence, and Luke shivered, swatting around his head as if trying to rid himself of pestering flies. Hoping it was only a stray, he descended the stairs to look for the animal. He quickly searched the entire ground floor but could find no trace of a wayward cat. The air around him had become heavy and clammy. He sensed, rather than saw, a cold wisp of something at the base of the stairs. Refusing to give in to his oncoming panic, Luke raced around the spot and up toward the room on the third floor. He wanted to pick up his tools and get the hell out of there!

Near the top of the staircase, he was sure he could hear light footsteps coming up behind him faster and faster, louder and louder. He forced himself to look over his shoulder. There was nothing there, but he felt a rotting breath on his face. His feet seemed fastened to the floor with drywall screws. He struggled to escape up the last few steps to the safety of the upper room.

Then he heard a muffled, heavy dripping as if something were oozing out of thin air onto the stairs. His whole body trembled. Goosebumps appeared on his arms. He climbed faster.

As he reached the third floor landing, a final sound floated up to him, this time a clear and distinct weeping. The hair on the back of his neck stood on end. His desire to run was overcome by an unhealthy need to see what was pursuing him. He couldn't help turning around.

His jaw dropped open.

MARY ELLEN

Mary Ellen looked up at the basement rafters where the axe her brother used to chop firewood hung motionless. It was shiny, sharp, gleaming...waiting. She reached out and touched it lightly, and it swung overhead like a scimitar. She took it down.

"That bastard thinks he has me? He'll see!"

She examined the tool, admired the razor sharp edge, and without another thought, raised it as high as she could and brought it down on her wrist with all the strength she had. She screamed as her severed hand flopped onto the floor. She grabbed an old oily rope and twisted it around her frayed stump until the bleeding slowed. She lifted up her severed hand and, with an insane cackle, stumbled up the three flights of stairs to the attic. All the way up, her severed limb dripped bright crimson blood on the rich mahogany risers.

She appeared at the window. George smiled in triumph. Then his smile turned to a rictus of horror. Mary Ellen, blood still dripping down one arm, held out her severed left hand and screamed, "Here is your ring back George! Perhaps you can give it to that tawdry sanitorium tart?"

Then Mary Ellen fainted.

LUKE

Coming up the bannister, gripping the railing and inching towards him, was a severed human hand, withered and mummified. Its skeletal fingers crept up the railing like a disembodied spider. On one of them, a fancy ring cast a ghostly shimmer.

A scream caught in Luke's throat and, gathering all his strength, he stumbled backward into the room. The weeping turned into a grinding shriek, and the entire top floor fell into a dark, cold pall. It was three stories up, but he pulled open the dormer window and crawled onto the narrow ledge outside. He could still hear the shrieking. He took a terrified look into the room and saw the ghastly hand inexorably crawling along the wall toward the window. His whole body shook as he gingerly crept around the dormer edge to the house's roof. When he reached the roof peak, he crawled all the way to the downspout.

He swung his body onto the spout and, hoping against hope it would hold his weight, started his descent. His legs wobbled as he tried to gain purchase. The loose pieces of gutter sliced into his hands. It started to creak as the ancient bands holding it to the house began to fail. Suddenly, Luke was airborne, plummeting towards the ground a full thirty feet below.

He landed on his back with a massive thud and lay stunned, looking up at the open window of Mary Ellen's bedroom. He tried to sit up, but felt no sensation in his legs. The screeching had stopped. It had been replaced by the feel of the withered old hand slowly gripping his throat and squeezing.

The last thing he heard was, "Once, I was happy!"

DEATH SMELLS A CERTAIN WAY

By George Mason

I KNEW SOMETHING WAS wrong even before I had my key in the door. Despite a mild alcoholic stupor, I was aware enough to notice that the door wasn't fully closed. A voice in the back of my head told me I shouldn't have stayed for a last drink, that I should have been home starting dinner for Karen. Marital crisis or not, we still had to eat, and over the years, it had fallen on me to be the family cook.

Ever since retiring from the Army, I couldn't seem to be on time for anything; a fact noted by my superiors in more than one performance review during my civilian days since. I think my managing director also said I was too *direct and raw* for executive communications. Their way of saying I hadn't quite adjusted my speech and manner to corporate America's desire to have bad news made to sound good.

Nevertheless, I arrived later than usual, and a troubling feeling overtook me as I looked at the door. All it took was an index finger to push the door open enough to step through and smell it. Death smells a certain way. When one walks into a room occupied by the recently deceased, they are greeted by the usual caustic smells of traumatic violence like burnt gunpowder, feces, urine and the *copper-esque* smell of blood. But there was something else. The feeling.

There are those of us who know when someone has passed. We can walk into a room and know something has happened there, whether an hour or a decade ago. We don't consider ourselves psychic, but we are able to use our senses in a way others have not yet discovered or developed. That is because everyone is psychic to a certain degree. When someone close to us passes, or more so when two *someones* pass, the feeling is even more present and powerful. It's not something I studied in the military police academy years before. It's something that we, as cops, picked up along the way.

And so, on a crisp October evening in Cincinnati, Nerissa Weingarten lay face up in a pool of her own blood, her surprise still visible on a beautiful face turned ashen and cold. One eye was closed, but the other half-open, as sometimes happens following the physical death. It took me a moment to accept what I was seeing. She hadn't deserved this. Forty-eight years old, she was just someone I passed at the club a few times, exchanging a smile or a greeting. With the body of a twenty-year-old college cheerleader, she turned every heterosexual male head. And because of my situation at home, I had begun to look forward to the smiles every morning.

I watched her a lot, just like every other guy at the club did. I would love to have been able to walk up and introduce myself, but she'd always been somewhat unapproachable. She worked out with an older guy who drove a black Volkswagen. About six foot two and one ninety, I thought at first he might be her father or an older brother or a coworker. He was at least my age, maybe older. Deep inside, though, I knew that there had to be something romantic between them. It was the way he touched her, and the way she responded to it. But for more than two years, I only saw them at a distance.

As was my habit then, I rode my bicycle to the gym every day weather permitted, but one day in June, a storm came up so fast that by the time I finished my workout, it was pouring.

I was on my way out, having passed the registration desk, when I spotted Nerissa in front of me. Oh, I suppose it might not have been as happenstance as that. I mean, I'd been noticing her more intently for several months. To tell the truth, my wife Karen and I had seen Nerissa and her guy around the area, taking quiet walks together. As I said, they always worked out together. Closely. I'd never seen two people who had so much to say to each other, and they seemed to be inseparable on the equipment. So, maybe subconsciously, I moved a little faster to the exit that day just because she was alone.

It was obvious to everyone that she was in much better shape than he. She would pound the treadmill like a woman possessed. He tended to work light weights at a slow pace and walk the treadmill next to hers while she ran. He usually pushed the machines one leg at a time, cautiously, like a man recovering from an illness or surgery. So, while he may not have been as focused on pushing his own limits, it was glaringly obvious he wanted to be close to her.

That was when it hit me, that one or both of them had to be married, and they were using the club as their meeting place. Even though neither wore rings, it made sense. I mean, they'd park in the corner of the parking lot, talking quietly around their cars. Every once in a while, Karen and I would see them taking those romantic, but seemingly innocent, walks along the bike paths or we'd catch them sneaking a hug when they thought no one was watching.

And so it began on that rainy day in June. Nerissa was by herself for a change, so I hastened to catch up to her. Then, a wondrous thing happened. As I bid a good morning to one of the club employees, I noticed that she slowed the pace of her exit. Then she stopped.

Could she have recognized my voice and actually been allowing me to catch up? Or was she not particularly keen on venturing out into a rainstorm and forestalling the inevitable drenching? For a brief moment I felt like the dog chasing cars, that wouldn't know what to do with one when he caught it.

"Wow," I said, somewhat predictably, "this is not going to be a fun ride home." I paused for a second. "Where's your . . . uh . . . partner today?"

She smiled. "Family issues."

My mind raced. This was it. This was the closest I'd ever been to a woman that I'd secretly desired from a distance for almost two years. Her smile was a little crooked, in the cutest way, and her brown eyes, while not giving anything away, were smiling too. The problem was that my brain was so dusty from twenty years of marriage that I was no longer good at interpreting signals.

I had not looked at another woman since the first date with my wife. And if another woman had flirted with me, I wouldn't have recognized it anyway. That receiver had simply been switched off. It wasn't recognizing or interpreting inbound signals. Those signals between two people taking a chance on the unknown and open to combat or enchantment.

Tragically, I don't remember much of our brief conversation that morning, except her suggesting, "I could throw your bike in my van and drive you home?"

Hell. This was a lady who innocently offered to help me out and the first thing my mind went to was not so innocent. But why now? Why after all these years was I starting to have these feelings?

It hadn't always been like that at home. When Karen and I first met, we enjoyed each other's differences. We were interested in each other. We were intrigued by each other. But, over the years, we fell into the rut of complacency and began to take each other for granted. In retrospect, our love was still there, somewhere, but our priorities in life had changed. She was a workaholic, and I fell into third or fourth place behind her job, kids and occasionally, her other family members.

The mental wheels raced hard that day. As we watched it pour outside, I thought about the problems that Karen and I had been having and the ramifications of her seeing me drive up in another woman's vehicle. I also considered that for the first time in twenty years how I desperately wanted to get into a van with the attractive woman. Not just to accept an innocent ride from a person whom I knew nothing about, but rather to get the raven-haired goddess alone so I could learn as much about her as possible in a six-minute ride home.

Maybe I could use the conversation to suggest an innocent follow-up meeting over coffee? For the first time in my marriage, I found myself attracted to someone else. It wasn't Nerissa Weingarten's fault. She just happened to have been in my space that day.

Some time back, I'd had a fencing instructor who'd said, "Relationships are a lot like fencing. They're about negotiation, but more importantly, about timing and distance. You have to be within the right distance at the right time before you can use your technique. And then you live or die."

Well, that was it. The timing had been right for the initial encounter, and we were certainly within an intimate distance. But I had long since abandoned any technique I might have had to interest or allure members of the opposite sex. And besides, I was approaching fifty and far too old for a raven-haired goddess who looked much younger than she had to be. So as a dozen questions raced through my mind, a cowardly survival mechanism kicked in, and I heard myself say to Nerissa Weingarten, "Oh, you're very sweet, but I probably need the exercise." With that, we both walked into the rain and went our separate ways.

Over the next three months, the situation with my wife continued to deteriorate. I sought an attorney to evaluate my options. The fact that I would talk to the lawyer before I discussed the situation with Karen would eventually prove to be the domino that set the fatalistic scenario into motion.

We tried to keep things cordial since our daughter Kelly was living with us at the time, and there was no reason to drag her into our drama. We handled the process the best we could until the mental health professional met with Karen. It was a requirement of the divorce process. She came home that night enraged and on the edge of losing control. I had never seen her like that. Even our daughter was concerned. This came as a complete surprise to me because my meeting had been the night before, and I actually felt better leaving the office.

From then on, things were more or less toxic in our home. And the best we could do as a couple was to just avoid speaking. As a matter of fact, we both began to find things to do so we were home together as little as possible. Sleeping was not an issue because she'd moved into another bedroom five years earlier, and like the lobster in cool water about to have the heat turned up, I had not noticed the gradual decline of the relationship over that time.

And so it went for a couple months until my cousin, recovering from surgery, told me how she was bored and needed something to do. I was still trying to grow my consulting business, and so I asked her to use her marketing resources to find eight or ten potential leads for my business. I was looking for small companies that did training and policy development in their own niche areas but would be open to adding certain security-related programs to their portfolios. Within a couple of days, she sent me a list of ten companies that fit the parameters I'd requested. Two in temporary staffing, a couple of law firms, a realty brokerage, and some small businesses that did not look at all promising for what I had in mind.

I poured a nice glass of single malt scotch and sat down at my computer to formulate a strategy to approach them. As if by divine intervention, the first on the list was Midwest Staffing, headquartered not far from where I lived. I pulled up their website and began to read. I clicked on the *About Us* page and saw her picture.

"Son of a bitch!" The words spontaneously came out of my mouth so loud Karen came into my office, somewhat annoyed, and asked if I was okay.

It was her. Nerissa Weingarten. My mind and heart raced as I responded to my wife, "It's okay. It's nothing."

I continued reading and then clicked on the *Contact Us* tab, and her email address jumped out at me as if it was the only text on the page. So, for the next thirty minutes, I drafted and re-drafted an introductory letter that sounded business-like but just personal enough to try to get her attention. After all, I didn't want to end up in her junk mailbox.

I knew she had received it because almost immediately I saw that she had checked my profile on several social media sites. I was ecstatic. I thought I might have broken through the casual surface and somehow gotten her to at least know me as more than a face at the club. It was the opportunity I'd been waiting for, to get a step closer to knowing her.

But then, for weeks, I heard nothing. No emails, no phone calls. I'd crossed a line. Maybe I exploited the situation and it backfired. As a matter of fact, on one subsequent visit to the club, I offered my customary greeting, and it appeared to catch her off guard. She fumbled to say hello, and rather than looking at me and smiling as she had, she looked down and away. For a behaviorist, this was a bad sign. I was never to know what caused that reaction, but by the following day, she was back to her old self. We traded smiles and made small talk.

My wife Karen had been a Special Agent with the FBI for more than twenty years but was still shy of the mandatory retirement age of fifty-seven by four years. She'd had some successful cases over the years and had been recognized for professionalism on several occasions. She was a good investigator, but when I met her, she was trying to get out of an abysmal relationship with a suicidal accountant who stalked her and anyone she went out with. That hadn't bothered me. On the contrary, I think that only interested me more. We were introduced by a mutual friend, who explained her situation to me and later stood up for us as my best man.

We were opposites. Opposites politically, opposites spiritually, and opposites about pretty much anything else that came up. It got to the point that I'd actually bait her on a topic of which I'd take the opinion contrary to my own, initially and aggressively, and wait for her to automatically go the other way. And then I'd have my fun and then agree with her. In the beginning, some of these arguments were challenging but fruitful. Later, they were just arguments.

Our differences gradually eroded the marriage. I likened it to swimming against the current at every turn, and when our youngest child Dan had finished college and become gainfully employed, I decided it was time to move on. I hadn't expected her to be so shocked. We had, after all, been sleeping in separate bedrooms for the past half-decade. I truly expected her to say, "What took you so long?"

Instead, what followed was a roller coaster of emotion ranging from anger to sadness to bargaining, and finally focusing back on anger. In twenty years, I had never seen her like that. She was convinced I had been keeping a girlfriend the past ten years, and she would not believe anything I told her. She went through my desk and files, and attempted to hack my computer. The trust was gone.

It was one night around the fire pit after we'd each had three drinks and an hour of sobbing that she said, "Please just tell me her name. Tell me her name, and I'll give you the divorce. I just need to know."

The truth was that there was no name to give her. But her sobs turned to screams, and she broke down and began to beg, and for some reason I believed I had to give her something to calm her down. She fell to her knees and began pulling on my shirt in hysterics. "Dammit! You promised me that we would never have secrets come between us! Tell me . . . please tell me!"

And in an instant of insanity, I heard myself mutter the word, *Nerissa*. It was the only name that came to mind. It was the only name that had been on my mind. Truth was she had absolutely nothing to do with my marital problems. She was just at the right time and place to make me realize it was time to move on and find someone new. "She's just someone I met at the club. We're not even dating."

Karen didn't believe anything I said anyway.

"This isn't over," she said, as she picked up her glass and went upstairs to bed. The following morning, she was back to being the cold and sarcastic roommate I had known for the past few months. She didn't mention the previous evening.

And so, a few hours later on a crisp October evening, I stood motionless in the doorway, looking at both of them on the floor of my living room. In the darkness, in peaceful repose. Karen's Sig P229 had left her grip but rested on the floor under the fingertips of her right hand. I'd never learn how she coaxed Nerissa to my house that night, but I would eventually piece together how she found her.

Bereft and humiliated, Karen could not accept that I was leaving her just to go a different direction with my life. She could not envision that there wasn't another person stealing me away from her. Enraged and out of her mind with grief, she had gone to the club and spoken to the manager. Using her tiny FBI badge, she managed to obtain a membership directory, and it didn't take long for her to find the only Nerissa in the list.

For twenty years, Karen was a superlative investigator, so I suppose it wouldn't have taken a lot of creativity to devise a plan to draw Nerissa to my house. I guess we'll never know what exactly was said. What the authorities do know is that Nerissa entered my house of her own free will. Her car had been parked on the street a couple of doors down, and had I been sober, I probably would have seen it immediately. Nevertheless, she entered and Karen was waiting with her duty weapon.

The criminalists said Nerissa was probably killed soon after entering the living room. Knowing Karen as I did, I would have expected some sort of lecture or confrontation first. It apparently didn't happen that way. After shooting Nerissa in the chest, as near as detectives could tell, Karen knelt down next to her and fired a single shot into her own temple. The star pattern indicating a contact wound was clearly visible. Karen fell forward, her head resting on Nerissa's left shin. Peaceful, yet macabre.

And that was it. With a couple of shots, she'd managed to punish me for my desires, my thoughts, and of course, my actions. She'd not sworn any kind of revenge, and I had not believed her capable of it. I mean, everyone swears revenge at one time or another, but they rarely act out. Who knows, maybe she was punishing the FBI for something as well.

As I looked at the two of them on the floor, forever joined by one act, my mind became blank. I wanted to cry, but I couldn't breathe. The images indelibly etched in my mind, I would always look back on that initial meeting and think, *What would have happened if I'd accepted that ride home in the rain?* Timing and distance.

I called the police and sat down on the couch, staring at the scene in front of me. They arrived in minutes, and were very courteous as they handcuffed me.

"Routine," one of them said, casually.

Sure, why not? I was the estranged husband, and statistically, the spouse is generally the first suspect. Especially when you admit you knew the other victim as well.

When we got to the police station, I called my attorney. He'd known Karen too, for a lot of years. He was totally shocked, of course. He sat beside me during questioning by a detective whose name I couldn't pronounce and no longer remember. It seems the detectives thought like Karen and also couldn't believe that I hadn't left my wife for someone else.

Neither could they believe that Nerissa and I were only passing acquaintances at the club. Acquaintances who might have developed a business or personal relationship at some point, had we been given the time. Timing and distance. Nevertheless, after going through my story, back to front and front to back a couple dozen times, they were able to verify that I'd been drinking heavily up the street at the time of death. Well, deaths.

After signing a stack of documents attesting to my willingness to sit through a Grand Jury hearing, my attorney picked up the manila envelope containing my possessions, and we walked into the night air. As I inhaled deeply he asked, "Where do you want me to take you? I mean, do you want to stop and pick up some clothes, or what?"

"I don't know, Mike." I inhaled. "I'm afraid I fall into that 'or what' category right now."

The officer on duty knew I was coming and allowed me inside to collect some of my clothes and toiletries. I paused on the way out to look into the living room. The bodies were gone, as were the shell casings and other evidence. All that remained were a couple of bloodstains on the carpet. I was sober by then, so the sergeant allowed me to take my car, and I drove to a hotel not far away, where I slept for almost a day.

Karen's memorial service was at ten o'clock a few days later. Nerissa's was at two, across town. Obviously, I had no right to intrude. But given the circumstances, and the fact that no one in her family knew me, there was no way I could not go and offer a silent apology to a woman that I had gotten killed by the careless drop of her name. The services were held in a small town where she grew up.

It was a moving tribute but because I had been emotionally drained for the past month, I hadn't shed a tear until the blond woman in her late fifties walked into the chapel, pushing a guy I recognized in a wheelchair. At first, I was taken by surprise, and I struggled to reconcile what I saw. It was Nerissa's Volkswagen guy, and the woman pushing him later introduced herself to me as Glynis, his wife. His name was Mike.

It turns out that he'd had a stroke a few years back and had gone to convalesce in a facility where Nerissa volunteered through her church. So it was only natural that they'd spent time together and become close. The doctors told him that he would in all likelihood have another more serious episode soon. Glynis told me Nerissa had taken a special interest in him and supervised his recovery, which included introducing him to the fitness regimen I witnessed at the club.

When he'd learned of Nerissa's passing, he suffered another minor stroke and should have remained in the hospital, but like me, he could not stay away. As we approached the casket, he looked at me and attempted a smile. He recognized me as someone who'd shared a memory of Nerissa. Maybe not the same kind of memory but a memory, nonetheless. He raised his right hand and I took it, the lump in my throat growing.

I had totally misjudged the situation. Their relationship had not been about forbidden lust, but of caring and compassion. We both looked at Nerissa for a minute, and when he broke down, Glynis wheeled him out of the chapel. I followed them out, because technically, I wasn't supposed to be there anyway.

It was in the parking lot next to their van that she told me the story. They really hadn't expected him to survive the first stroke, but the support and nurturing of his caregivers seemed to light a spark in his eyes. It was the same spark I'd seen so many times at the club when I'd say hello to him. In all that time, it never occurred to me that even though he would smile, he never said one single word to me. Words were not easy for him. Their furtive meetings were nothing more than the attempt to avoid the appearance of impropriety. They were both respected in their church and did not want to start any vicious gossip about their activities.

I helped her get him into the car for the lonely ride home. It's always lonely for the living. The dead have somewhere else to be. As their taillights turned out of the parking lot and disappeared from view, I thought about returning to the chapel for one last look but dismissed the idea. That was no longer Nerissa in there. The life was gone. The body in the box was nothing more than a wax replica of a human who once shared her life with others.

It was all about timing and distance. Thrust, parry . . . whatever. What if I had accepted Nerissa's offer of a ride that day? What if I had met her three years earlier? What if I had never mentioned her name, or waited until her presumed relationship with Mike had run its course and she was ready to start dating again? What if the world was really flat, after all?

I was never to see Glynis or Mike again. A couple weeks later when I opened the obituary section of the newspaper, my eyes immediately froze on his picture. Mike Ruthven, age sixty, passed away quietly in his home Saturday, following a lengthy illness.

Mike and Nerissa were together again.

27 CROSSROADS DRIVE

By Thomas Brown

JIM ROLLED ONTO HIS back and stretched. He could feel it was the last morning of the month as much as he knew it. It always gave him a sick, queasy feeling.

He ran his fingers through his shoulder-length brown hair and looked at the tall cool one, still asleep next to him. His Boon. He watched her breathe, her chest rising and falling slowly, and he wondered what she dreamed of. Did she dream at all? She reminded him of a model he'd met in a dream of his own, somewhere along Hollywood Boulevard, maybe in '67. Maybe not.

Time and history were vague, and he preferred it that way. You couldn't lose something, someone, if you couldn't remember shit.

He rolled out of bed and slid his leather pants on. He had a closet full of them, along with long silk shirts, black leather boots. Once a month an outfit from the closet found his touch. The rest of the time jeans and a t-shirt were where it was at. But the last day of the month had its expectations. The Lizard King didn't wear jeans. So he put on his boots and walked on down the hall, yeah.

The house was enormous; he was never certain how many people lived with him, but it didn't matter. Jim always sought out the same people—people to listen to his ideas, his poetry, his bullshit.

At the bottom of the grand staircase was the entryway to the house; one of the many kitchens was nearby. He'd woken up that morning and gotten himself a beer. He had the urge to repeat the sentence in his head, and it made him smile. The end of the month always made him nostalgic. The can was cold, and beer spit on his hand as he popped the top.

His boots led him past the ancient gallery, full of masks. He wondered what his house mates saw in the room, what they saw as they wandered through the house. He knew the experience wasn't uniform. Creativity didn't work that way.

The room was full of lost imagination, an ever-changing muse to inspire the mind and make the pen flow. Jim didn't need it, so the room played games with him, fucking with his too sober mind. It didn't have to be that way, said the devil, always on his shoulder, somewhere in his head.

Nah, he'd rather be sober than alone.

Notes of music chewed holes in the air, and his boots led him somewhere else. He gravitated to music, always had, and his boots led him to the porch. The screen door separated the in from the out, and Jim kicked the door open, the wooden porch creaking under his weight.

The porch made a sound he knew from when he was a kid. The three boards leading to the front door of his house in Texas always let his mother know when he was coming or going. The boards didn't bend or break no matter how often he stepped on them, but the sound was unmistakable and vaguely comforting.

A pair of guitars jammed together, the two men playing off each other, and Jim did a little shimmy as he joined them outside. Robert was running his impossibly long, nimble fingers along the guitar's strings, making sound come from it that his many friends and admirers had spent their lives imitating. He had on his dark brown suit and matching fedora. He'd been photographed in the suit once. It was his end of the month suit.

Robert Johnson would dress to the nines for the ladies, once upon a time. Now he dressed to impress for the monthly meeting of nostalgia.

Jimi sat next to him, his Stratocaster strung upside down for his left-handed playing. They shared the first joint of the day, and Robert offered him a toke, but Jim shook his head.

"Nah man, I'm cool, thanks," said Jim in his always drifting, going somewhere else voice.

"It must be the motherfucking last day of the month," said Robert. But he knew it himself. He didn't fall out of bed in that suit.

"I bet you already have next month's written, and the one after that."

Robert and Jimi both laughed, knowing they were exactly the same. Robert handed the roach over to Jimi, who tucked it in the corner of his mouth as he worked out the key for some future piece.

Jim stared out at the yard in front of him. It was still morning, but it was scorching on the lawn, the waves of heat vibrating and flexing the very air in front of him.

"Was it ever this hot in the delta, Rob?" Jim watched the long fingers slide along the bridge of the guitar, entranced by the ease with which they glided down the strings.

"There's hot, James, and there's last day of the month hot. Last day of the month always hotter than the hottest day on the Delta. Hottest day anywhere. Is Janney done yet?" He knew the answer just like Jim did. There was a solidarity in the house. No one wanted anyone else to fail, to disappoint.

"You know she isn't. I'm headed back to talk to her now. She's probably high as a kite with Amy, if she's gotten up at all. See you boys for lunch."

Both guitars strummed a goodbye, and Jim wandered back into the house looking for Janney. There were several great rooms, filled with instruments, recording devices, microphones, and speakers. People would play at all hours of the day and night, whenever inspiration hit them.

But Janney had long ago lost her inspiration and gone from last minute to not at all. Others in the group had pretended to write for her, but the Boss knew. There was only one of her, which was of course why she lived in the house with them. They all shared the disease of never-ending creativity. It was that creativity that paid the rent, fed them, clothed them, and gave them their monthly Boon.

Janney's Boon was a familiar one, the one from the beginning that she had a permanent romance with. It was her muse, her love, mistaken intention, her eternal loss.

It was smack.

Good and pure, a spike of never-ending heat that numbed her from the world. Forever and a day. It had poisoned her spirit, eaten her soul. She'd struggled with it for so many years, but until recently it had never gotten in the way. Now she just liked to get wasted and start fights, instead of caring about the one responsibility she had. Write a song, a poem, a story, even a fucking limerick.

She had his sympathy. Once upon a time he too had forsaken the grip reality held on him for the warm embrace of heroin. He'd loved her more than any mistress or girlfriend he had known. But she'd betrayed him; it was simply in her nature. So given the choice, he had long preferred the embrace of the living.

Sort of.

So, Jim wrote eight or ten poems or songs a month. He always had something to say.

Jim found Janney stretched out on a couch with the TV running loud enough to wake the dead and turned it down at the knob. Though he had seen others use something called a remote, he could never find it. He sat down next to his friend and ran his fingers through her hair. Her eyes were glazed over from not blinking for several minutes, and Jim wasn't certain if she knew he was even there. She was wearing the same outfit she had been wearing for days. She smelled bad, and in a house full of musicians who never had the best hygiene habits, that was saying something.

"You seem all set to call the Boss's bluff, Janney." Jim already had ideas in mind, he just needed her throaty flair added to it.

She blinked. Her eyes rolled around behind their lids, re-lubricating them.

"Bingo. And it's Janis. It's the last day of the month, ain't it." Spite filled her words. It was the sound that came from a desire to harm someone with her acid wit. There was a certainty, based just on the day, who it was. "Let the bastard come."

That was that, and Jim knew it. A tug, a pull, filled him from the base of his spine, from the pit of his stomach.

Janney got up. She felt it too. It was a call no one could ignore. Both of them wandered into the great room and saw most of the house was already there.

The Boss was there too, sitting behind a card table with a stack of papers at the front, like the reports all of them turned into the teacher at school.

So, so similar. He smiled at both Jim and Janney, polite and warm. Jim reached into his back pocket, unfolded an eight-stanza poem, and added it to the stack. Janney came next and flicked her finger at the Boss before sitting down next to Jim on a couch.

"All right. This month looks to be almost complete. I have just signed a new band to our label, and I appreciate all the music you have contributed to their success." The Boss looked happy with himself, in his white linen suit and slicked back hair.

"Their name is 'Pretend Weekend,' and I have signed the entire band. So, I have to keep my word and give them something to perform because they can't be relied on to do it themselves."

"Any of them joining us?" asked Robert, slurring his words, his guitar resting under his arm.

"Oh no, Robert. But as you well know, if they were a complete package, they wouldn't have signed with me. Just like all of you, they are missing something. Just as all of you would have gotten there anyway if you had been born with some patience, so thank Dad for not giving it to you. Anyway, is there anyone who wants a different Boon, Jim? Are you tiring of them, there are so many other things out there?"

"No thank you, man. I'm good." Jim just wanted it to end, for the Boss to leave again. A few of the others changed things up, and then it was done.

"Janis, Janis, Janis. What am I to do with you? The sweat of your brow, the sound of your voice, these are the things that pay your way. I wasn't joking last month. So, you have no Boon this month." The Boss snapped his fingers.

Jim looked at his friend and realized Janney was sober and wide awake. She could see the world for what it was, no hiding.

Tears streamed down her face. She didn't have the gnawing pain or the hunger. No, this was worse. She was as clean as the day she was born. She knew where she was, why, and how long she had been there. She knew there was nothing to hide behind, no distraction that would be enough.

The Boss stood and put on his matching fedora. He picked up his stack of papers and slid them into his briefcase. "Kurt, that is a particularly catchy little ditty. If the world knew you wrote that instead of one of my fools, they would go crazy. Outstanding job." Kurt nodded his shaggy blond head as the Boss got ready to leave.

Jim followed him to the front door. "Boss come on, man. She just needs a break. She's never taken to the house like most of the rest of us, she's too tightly wound for this place."

"Jim, you were such a selfish bastard when I met you, who would have thought you would become this. Janis will learn. There's no other way." The Boss stepped out onto the porch as waves of heat swirled around the house.

He stopped as the Boss stepped into the swirling convection. Jim would catch fire in such heat. The Boss waved to Jim, ignoring the heat that would melt a soul. "You're such a softy, Jim. You know there is always a charge here. There is always hell to pay. See you next month."

And then he was gone.

PYRACANTHA

By J. Powell Ogden

DAY 6

"DO YOU SEE IT?" Frank hunched down low in the old truck's passenger seat, head below the window. He gritted his teeth to stifle a groan. "Is it coming?"

"Are you okay?" Charlene searched him frantically with her eyes. One leg of his jeans was ripped above his muddy bare foot. There was blood. "Did it get you?"

"Goddamn it, Charlene! Is it coming?"

Crouching on the driver's side, Charlene slid upward and peeked out the window at the rundown farmhouse. The front door gaped under the new moon. Her heart beat a warning drum in her ears.

"No. I don't think—"

Gravel crunched and slid on the other side of the passenger door. Dread sank down Charlene's spine. She mouthed, "It's on your side."

Frank started to inch up to see.

She grabbed his sweaty hand and pulled him down. "Don't."

He yanked his hand free and inched up higher, but stopped suddenly and buried his hands in his hair. He turned toward her, eyes wide, terrified.

"Chuck…I can't see."

DAY 1

"It's called *Pyracantha*," the real estate agent said. "Firethorn. Because of the berries."

Charlene had wanted a blackberry farm. Her Great Aunt Hilda had a dairy farm with wild blackberry bushes tucked into the woods at the edge of the pasture behind the farm's electric fence. When Charlene was small, she climbed carefully through the two zappy wires and picked berries, stuffing them into her mouth until her fingers and lips were stained purple.

Now, at thirty, Charlene had the electric fence, the pasture and the barn, but no blackberries. Instead, she stared up at the most hideous, orange-berried monstrosity she had ever seen. The thorny hedge, planted parallel to the front of the farmhouse, topped ten feet tall and stretched at least fifty feet on either side of a rusty iron gate. The gate, which was nearly as tall as the hedge and barely wide enough to squeeze a truck through, separated the farm's rutted access road from its gravel parking area and long, arching dirt driveway.

Charlene had known the hedge would be here. It was here when she toured the place. It was here when she bought it. But somehow she hoped it would be gone the day she moved in. Standing with Helene Harper, their real estate agent, Charlene peered through the cobwebby gate at the house. A drop of late summer sweat trickled down her back between her shoulder blades. She looked over her shoulder at Frank, who was tugging a forty-eight pack of the thinnest, shittiest toilet paper ever out of the back of their Subaru, which was parked behind their rented U-Haul.

She told him, "This thing's gone in the spring. We'll plant sunflowers."

"We'll need a chainsaw."

"Or a bulldozer, François. Let's buy a bulldozer."

"Sure, Chuck. In the spring."

He pulled out a second forty-eight pack of toilet paper and stacked it on the gravel beside the first. He crawled into the back of the Subaru, his ass disappearing as he reached for the third. That ass filled out his jeans nicely. That ass, Charlene loved. She knew she was lucky it was here. Frank hadn't wanted to move out to the country surrounded by dirt, domestic critters and wild things. For him, country living meant a stack of pancakes at The Cheese Bucket, Frank's vernacular for The Cracker Barrel. Frank was here for one reason only—okay, maybe two because, yeah, he loved her—but the second reason was—

BOOM!

Charlene ducked, tripping backward into Helene. The agent's pretty spike heels slid through the gravel, but she was solid, heading into chunkster territory, and she grabbed Charlene under her arms to keep her upright.

That was no gunshot. Charlene knew guns, and that was no—

CRACK! CRACK!

Now, those were gunshots. Semi-automatic rifle fire she was sure. The shots came from behind the house, maybe the next farm over.

Frank scrambled out of the back of the Subaru, sweaty hair askew. "What the hell was that?"

"Tannerite," Helene said. She smoothed her navy suit jacket down and smiled almost apologetically. "Your neighbor, Boone Pritchard." She sighed. "He likes to blow things up. Tannerite is a—"

BOOM!

Charlene's fillings rattled.

"—kind of exploding target for shooting practice. Here are your keys." She held them up so they gleamed in the hot August sun. Charlene didn't take them. She was still processing the explosions. The agent gave them a little shake, and Frank walked over and took them from her hand.

"Thank you, Helene."

"You're welcome." She smiled brighter. "Tannerite's expensive. Boone will run out soon. Enjoy!" Helene's truck tires spun on the gravel, spraying up dust as she beat a hasty retreat.

Frank held up the keys and grinned. "The keys to your dream home."

BOOM! BOOM!

He startled. "Oh, shit!"

Charlene laughed. "I promised you a safe house far from the big bad city germs, not quiet."

BOOM!

Frank shook his head, still grinning. "Oh, it's not quiet, Chuck."

She propped her hands on her hips. "Frank."

He tossed her the keys and scooped up his toilet paper. "Come on. Let's go check 'er out."

Charlene followed him through the gate and up the porch steps. The two-story farmhouse was built in 1904 and sat on thirty-eight acres of rolling pasture and old growth forest. Its white paint was flaking off, half the windows were fogged or painted shut and the roof sagged near the chimney. It was still her dream home, because beyond the house, beside their small, dappled wood, was a riding ring and a sturdy barn with four stalls. Tomorrow, two of those stalls would be occupied. Her Quarter Horses, June and Cash, were coming home.

The long thrumming call of a cicada drifted lazily on the warm, humid breeze. Charlene knocked a stink bug off the door knob, fit the key in the lock and pushed open the front door. The house was just like it had been during the final walk through—dated pea green carpet in the parlor, scuffed wood floors in the foyer, dining room and kitchen, and ropy vine and flower wallpaper on every stinkin' wall. The house smelled musty, and she detected the faint aroma of cat urine, but those smells would go when the carpet and hideous wallpaper were gone.

Frank kissed her on the cheek, murmuring *dream home* in her ear as he passed her. She smiled. He cut left around the heavy oak bannister and jogged up the steps with his giant pack of toilet paper. The steps and upstairs floorboards creaked as he circled back toward the bedroom at the front of the house. That room was Frank's designated "bomb shelter." Obviously, a bomb shelter should be in a basement to protect it from bombs and tornadoes and the like, but the house didn't have one. It had a cellar with alcoves full of dank dirt and creepy spiders. Frank hated spiders, but germs were more likely to kill you, which was the second reason he'd agreed to the move to "the country."

Frank was a medical coder, and medical coders knew the code for every injury, surgery and disease that ever existed. Frank was especially drawn to infectious diseases. Call it a genetic abnormality. His favorite movie was *Outbreak*. His favorite video game was *Resident Evil Zero,* which he'd *finally* purchased. His favorite pastime was developing marginally edible recipes using shelf-stable foods.

Ebola.

SARS.

Influenzas A, B, C and Double D.

With the deadly SARS outbreak of 2002 only recently winding down, Frank was sure the next plague was coming. No one knew when, he'd said, but it could be worse than the Spanish Flu or the Black Death, and this little farmhouse of theirs checked off a few boxes on his pandemic preparedness wish list. It was remote, had well water, a diesel generator, and lots of storage space. It was short a few, too, namely, mechanical soundness, cleanliness and a rifle. Charlene was ready to clean and repair, but guns were a nonstarter. She knew guns, and there would be no gun in her house. Ever.

Frank loped back down the stairs. "Get a move on, Chuck. We only got a few hours of daylight left, and they say it's gonna storm later." He goosed her ass as he passed.

"Damn it, Frank!"

After wrestling their boxes and sparse cache of furniture out of the U-Haul and into the house, the two sat grimy, sweaty and starving on an old quilt on their four-poster bed. The tools they'd used to put the antique together lay haphazard on the floor under the window. A small, pink plastic cooler sat on the bed between them. Frank had packed a picnic—not shelf stable, thank God. Fried chicken, chips, coleslaw and Twinkies. There were no napkins, and the paper towels were downstairs, much too far to fetch, so Charlene had resorted to licking her fingers as necessary and wiping them on her shirt.

"Ugh, Chuck. Germs!"

"Just my germs, François. The house has been empty for weeks, so…"

"So…a prairie dog might have broken in here."

"A prairie dog."

"Yes, Chuck."

"In Ohio."

"They carry Monkeypox. Very nasty." A warm night breeze blew in through the open window and torn screen behind him, stirring his dark curly hair. "Two years ago there were several cases."

"Seriously?"

"Absolutely."

A teasing grin spread over Charlene's lips. "I love it when you talk diseases to me, François."

"You do, do you?" He pulled the chicken leg Charlene was gnawing on out of her hand and dumped it in the cooler, then picked up the cooler and set it on the floor by the tools. He leaned in to touch her grubby, moving-day lips with the tip of his greasy finger. "Damn the germs then."

She sucked his finger into her mouth, circling it with her tongue. Frank dragged her up onto his lap and plucked his finger out of her mouth so he could kiss her properly. His lips tasted like dust, sweat and fried chicken.

Thunder rumbled in the distance.

"Guess the storm's here," he whispered.

"Guess it is."

Frank tugged the hair tie off her long, messy ponytail and wove his fingers into her hair. Thunder rolled again. A flash of faint, diffuse lightning brightened the sky outside their window. The back of Charlene's neck prickled, which made the kissing more intense. She slid off Frank's lap and stretched out beside him, tugging him with her.

Another ripple of thunder, closer. She slipped her hand up under his shirt.

"Mmmm," he murmured, returning the favor.

A deafening crack rocked the house, vibrating the bed. The window lit up like a white hot fireball. Frank jerked away from her and rolled off the bed, hitting the ground hard on his side. Charlene stumbled through the tools on her way to the window, stubbing her baby toe as she went. Her eyes smarted. Her toe throbbed. But she was preoccupied by the flames and smoke billowing up from their wood out back. She smelled ozone. The wind rose, fanning the flames higher. Charlene dug through her backpack on the floor for her brand new flip phone to call the fire department.

The whole house shook as the downpour began.

It was still pouring when the firefighters arrived. Charlene and Frank walked with them out to the woods through the weeds and the mud under umbrellas that were all but useless in the gusty wet wind. Of course, the rain had put the fire out. In storm slickers, the firefighters inspected the damage. A few scorched trees and downed limbs. Dirt, still steaming, had been thrown in an arc at least a dozen meters from where the bolt hit the ground, leaving a crater full of water and mud behind. Charlene hadn't known lightning could do that.

"It travels through the roots," the fireman said, rain pouring off his white helmet. "Kicks up all the dirt above them like a bomb going off."

Charlene was glad June and Cash hadn't arrived yet. They might have kicked right through their stalls.

DAY 2

It was still raining the next morning when Charlene reached through the bars of the iron gate to unhook a thorny *Pyracantha* branch from the rear bumper of the trailer carrying her horses. It had taken Danny, the driver, six tries to thread the truck and trailer through the narrow gate. Now it seemed the nasty hedge itself was pissed he had succeeded.

"Careful," Danny warned through his open window. "The sap on those thorns stings."

"Got it." She looped her finger gingerly around the woody twig between pinky-long spikes and dragged it off. "You're good to go." She stood up in her dripping rain slicker and followed the trailer as it bumped and rumbled through the mud on its way back to the barn.

After leading him into his stall, Charlene rubbed Cash's velvety muzzle. "Hi, old man," she crooned. The twenty-year-old Quarter Horse was head-to-toe glossy black, fifteen hands high, and gentle as they came. Charlene intended to teach riding once they were settled, and Cash would be the perfect lesson horse. June, on the other hand, was a gorgeous, but spirited, Buckskin. Golden brown with a rich dark mane. As she and Danny tugged the young mare out of the trailer, the horse stomped and reared up, splattering mud on her satiny coat and all over Charlene's jeans.

"Stop that!" Charlene yanked hard on her halter. "Stop it, June." June snorted before swinging her head around to bump her nose into Charlene's chest. "Be nice, June." Charlene rubbed the white blaze on her face. June nickered. "You miss me? Yeah, you missed me." She pulled a sugar cube out of her pocket and fed it to her on a flat palm.

Pretty June wouldn't be giving lessons. The show horse needed training, and Charlene couldn't wait to dig in.

"It's perfect, ain't it?" Danny said, admiring her soggy property. His face had wizened to old leather from years out in the weather. Danny had boarded Charlene's horses for years, and he was happy for her. "You want me to put out the word? You lookin' to board horses in them two extra stalls?"

"Just one," Charlene said, lifting a pile of hay and tossing it into June's stall. "I'm buying another lesson horse. You could look out for that."

"Sure thing. Gonna miss you, Chuck."

Chuck.

Frank's nickname for her had caught on and stuck over a decade ago when she'd first started teaching. Frank, a gangly kid with loose dark curls and expressive eyes, had been one of her first pupils. He teased her mercilessly during the ten beginner lessons his mother made him take—only to decide horses were too damn big, stinky and scary to keep at it. Charlene had been fifteen. Frank had been fourteen. The lessons were cheap and shouldn't have come with the girl, but she was smitten. The two had been together ever since.

Charlene tossed some hay into Cash's stall, donned her raincoat and headed back out into the rainy morning. Off in the woods to her left, the mud still steamed near the site of the lightning strike, and she wondered if decomposing leaves below the forest floor were still burning. She sniffed the air. She only smelled damp, wet earth, but she'd seen stacks of hay bales smolder from the inside out until one day the whole pile went up in flames. She made a mental note to keep an eye on it.

In the mudroom, she kicked off her dirty boots and jeans and trudged up the stairs to shower, but took a quick, barefoot detour to look in on Frank in his bomb shelter. Over half the front bedroom was taken up by his "stash." There were stacks of toilet paper, paper towels and cleaning products. Shelves of boxed foods and staples like flour, sugar and yeast, cans of fruit and vegetables. A wind-up radio, flashlight and mini-fridge. Clear plastic bins full of first aid supplies, over-the-counter medications and a few she was sure required a prescription. He hadn't told her who had written those scripts, and she hadn't asked him. Frank was her mysterious little Plague Prepper. Her hero-in-waiting.

"Hungry?"

Sitting at his desk, Frank absently waved her off as he squinted through his glasses at the monitor of his new desktop computer. Frank was deep in the zone, translating doctors' chicken scrawl into the codes hospitals used to bill for patient care. With his talent for hyper-focusing, he was good at his job, though she didn't understand how he could spend eight hours a day locked up inside with his eyes glued to a screen. She glanced down at her bare legs and thought of her muddy pants in the utility sink.

Charlene smiled. He didn't always understand her either.

She walked down the hall and pushed open the pocket door separating their bedroom from the master bath. The five foot wide door, with its shiny, recessed oak panels, was almost a work of art. The bathroom behind it, with its solid oak cabinet and double marble sink, old fashioned laundry chute, claw-foot tub and circular curtain rod suspended above it, might have been beautiful, too, if it had escaped the frilly, cloying wallpaper. Alas, even the ceiling had not been spared.

Charlene pushed the half-unpacked boxes out of the way, stripped, turned on the shower and gave a satisfied sigh. The water pressure was strong, and really, that's all that counted, right? When she stepped out of the tub, she opened the cabinet under the sinks and reached for a towel, but yanked her hand back. A trail of what looked like black grains of rice lay scattered around the trash can. The can was full of chicken bones and Twinkie wrappers. She wrinkled her nose.

Mouse droppings.

Charlene quickly mopped them up with a wad of toilet paper and flushed them, hoping it was just one hungry mouse, but she knew better. If a mouse was all the way up on the second floor looking for food, there were more in the cellar.

And Frank would want to kill them all.

Mice carried disease.

When they found mice in their last house, Frank bought at least two dozen traps, the kind you baited with peanut butter, and had set them all over the house. He checked them in the morning before Charlene got up. Every day she would ask if he caught any, and every day he said no. Then one day, she'd knocked a trap over while mopping. On the back side of the wood, Frank had penciled three small mouse heads with "X's" for eyes. Three dead mice.

Suddenly dizzy, Charlene sat on the floor with her dripping back against the cool pocket door as the memory of another small, furry dead thing lurched into her mind. That creature had screamed so loud…before.

She wiped her hands on her naked wet thighs. No. Frank didn't need to know about the mice yet. Maybe if she cleaned really well and put all their food in air tight containers, the little guys would head back into the fields.

Charlene snatched a towel from under the sink, dried off and quickly dressed. She resolved to mop, scrub and dust the place from roof to cellar, but before that, she would search the house, the yard and the barn to make sure no traps or rat poison had been left behind by the previous owner. She should have done that before the horses arrived.

That night, with the sound of the rain still beating against their roof, she fell asleep with her head on Frank's chest while he paged through his latest comic, *Apocalyptic Zombie Doomsday No. 4*. She'd worked hard all day, and her hands were red and raw from scrubbing, but she was satisfied. She'd found no traps, no poison. The mice were safe.

A faint clicking sound woke her after midnight.

Sitting up in bed, she brushed her hair out of her eyes and

listened, but the sound had stopped. She glanced over at Frank. The room was silent. The rain had finally ended and a sliver of cool blue moonlight fell across his shoulders. She pulled the sheet up to cover him, then shuffled toward the bathroom, sliding the pocket door shut behind her. In the moonlight, the creepy vines on the wallpaper unwound and crawled all over the walls. Charlene shivered and switched on the glaring overhead light, which was almost worse. After washing up, she heard the odd clicking again followed by a rustling sound near the other sink drain.

Well, shit.

She slowly leaned over the drain, tense and vaguely worried something might crawl out of it. She squinted one eye shut. Nothing. Only the light reflected back up at her from the water deep in the trap.

Click, click...*click.*

It was underneath the sink.

She crouched and cautiously opened the cabinet door, scooching back a bit. If the mouse was back, Charlene didn't want it scurrying over her bare feet. The explosive flurry of slippery movement confronting her was not what she expected, and she toppled over backward, landing on her tailbone. Disoriented, she rubbed the heels of her hands against her eyelids until she saw stars. When the stars faded, there was only a messy stack of towels, an empty trash can, and a dark, gnawed, hand-sized hole in the back of the cabinet.

Charlene stood up and gave a soft laugh. It was just a mouse. She switched off the light, and the creeping vines of the wallpaper closed back in.

The old house had her seeing things.

DAY 3

Charlene tugged the brim of her ratty Carhartt baseball cap down low on her sweaty forehead. She held the lunge line firmly as she worked June in a circle around the riding ring, trying to knock some of the stubbornness out of her. Clouds lounged lazy and steamy white in the blue afternoon sky high above, and the scent of heavy wet earth, leather and perspiring horse filled her nose. Flies landed on June's back, buzzing and biting. June swished her black tail.

"Let's go, June." She clicked her tongue. "Get." June was more interested in eating the tufts of grass in the muddy dirt at her feet. Charlene added weeding to her already long list of chores. "Let's go, June!" She gave the whip a snap. June bucked, her hind legs throwing up sticky dirt clods, and then pranced, picking her dainty feet up high. Her thick black mane billowed out behind her. "Nice! So pretty, June!" Charlene smiled. June was only two and a half, but Charlene could already tell when she was all trained up, she was going to be a showstopper.

"That's enough." Charlene dug a sugar cube out of her pocket, and June snagged it with her warm, wet lips. Charlene rubbed her prickly nose. "Good job, Junie bug."

Charlene turned her out in the electric-fenced field on the

other side of the barn. She turned Cash out, too, and headed back to the house.

Sitting on the back stoop, Charlene dragged off her muddy cowboy boots and socks and paused to soak in the view. The previous owner had let the grass between the backyard fence and the riding ring go wild. Native Ohio prairie grasses and wildflowers stood chest high in places, and yellow finches and dragonflies hovered and dipped above them. Pretty garden spiders as big as your hand had stretched their webs between them. In the distance, her land rolled into neighboring farms and woods. The property was breathtaking, and she still couldn't believe it was hers.

Charlene slapped at a mosquito on her cheek and stood, ready to get back to unpacking, but something at the edge of her shadow caught her attention. A small furry thing. Very still. Her breath caught.

Aw, crap. A dead mouse.

She'd have to get rid of it before Frank saw it.

She found a stick and padded over on bare feet. She squatted and prodded it with the stick. The poor little thing had matted fur and an open wound on one of its hind legs, buzzing with gnats. Her stomach rolled. She looked away and then back, steeling herself. She flipped it over. Gnats buzzed around its dead eyes, too, which had weird bloody circles around them. She leaned in for a closer look.

"Whatcha got there?"

The voice was unfamiliar, wet and wheezy. A long shadow

fell over her. Charlene stood, startled, and turned. The man standing there was tall and lanky. Despite the heat, he wore a blue chambray shirt buttoned up to his chin, sleeves rolled down and cuffs buttoned at his wrists. His saggy jeans were cinched at his waist with a warped leather belt and a near Frisbee-sized belt buckle. That buckle held her attention in its godawful grip. Fangs. Rattlesnake fangs. The snake's mouth hinged wide open, ready to strike. Its body and rattle were wrapped around the word TEXAS spelled out in Texas-sized letters. All caps.

The man moved in front of her. "That a mouse?"

"No." Charlene reflexively kicked the dead thing with her bare foot into the tall weeds behind her, flinching at the feel of its cold, stiff body rolling off her toes. "Who—?"

"I knocked on yer door." He waved over the barn. "I live behind ya back there. Boone Pritchard."

Oh Lord. The man who liked to blow things up.

Charlene took a long step back. "Mr. Pritchard—"

"Have ya seen any of my chickens? Little Orpies. Fluffy white? I'm down to two. Glock, Wesley and Smith is missin'. They don't usually wander."

Boone's chickens might not wander, but his eyes certainly did. He was talking to her, but he was looking past her.

"No," she said. "Sorry. I'm kinda busy, so…"

Boone stepped around her, and she caught a heady whiff of dip. A black dab of the stuff clung to the scraggly whiskers on his chin. "Mice, huh?" He pointed at the house's foundation. "You got a few holes there. More likely chipmunks. Voles. You know they dig away at the foundation. They keep diggin' and diggin' and one day it all falls in. I seen it. Family lost a house on County 4 a few years back. I got some bait back at the house. Anticoagulant. The good stuff."

The last thing Charlene wanted to do at the moment was discuss all the ways to snuff out small rodents with her strange, overeager, gun-blasting new neighbor. She smiled politely, though, while she brainstormed ways to effect his speedy departure.

"Oh, I couldn't—"

The screen door creaked open behind her.

"Hello, who's this?"

Her heart sung with gratitude. Her rescuer stood in the doorway. Frank wasn't a big man, but he was a bright one. He noted her posture, the cringe on her face and stepped out, putting his body between Charlene and Boone. He stuck out his hand. "I'm Frank Boucher. You gotta name, man?"

"Boone Pritchard."

Frank looked at Charlene.

Yup. The man who liked to blow things up.

Boone shook Frank's hand firmly. "Just lookin' for a few of my white chickens. Glock, Wesley and Smith. Red comb a'top their heads? Real fluffy."

Frank glanced around the yard. "No chickens here, buddy." He looked at Boone expectantly.

"I know. Thanks. Yer wife told me." Boone hooked his thumbs through his belt loops, unhurried. "I see you got yourself a rodent problem, Frank. I'm kinda the neighborhood expert on critter removal. I got some bait. Anticoagulant. It kills ‘em by—”

“Oh, I know what anticoagulants do.” Still talking, Frank walked toward the side of the house, forcing Boone to follow him. “They bleed out.” Frank actually sounded interested in the topic, and Boone chased after him.

“It’s the best kind.”

“You think so?”

The two disappeared around the corner leaving Charlene alone.

The sun had sunk lower in the sky, and the shade of the tall prairie grass now stretched halfway across the yard. Charlene heard a crunching sound near the fence, near where she had kicked the dead mouse. Wildflowers shimmied back and forth. In spite of the heat, gooseflesh rose on her arms. She gave the yard a last glance and retreated into the house.

Hours later, sitting on the front porch steps, Frank sliced a piece off his apple and handed it to Charlene. The moon was up, just a sliver, and the bats were out, circling and swooping above them, scooping bugs out of the sky. Frank smacked a fat mosquito on his forearm. It exploded, leaving a bloody red splotch behind.

“Ick,” Frank grumbled, rubbing it off. “Hello, West Nile. Gimme the bug spray.”

Charlene did, and he sprayed his arms, the back of his neck and then a pungent cloud all around them. Charlene coughed.

They listened to the crickets and stared into the depths of their Firethorn border wall.

"You can't even see the road," Charlene said. "We live in a fortress."

"With cannons out back," Frank said.

"Oh my God," Charlene laughed. "That guy's a—"

"Probable inbred."

Charlene shoved him. "You're horrible!"

He stared out at the bush, trying to keep a straight face, then burst out laughing.

She pummeled his arm with her fists. "Stop! He's just… socially challenged."

"Okay! You're right! He's the perfect neighbor!" He hooked an arm around her. "This place is incredible, Chuck. It really is." And the way he said it, she knew he was happy, and that made her feel warm. Then he looked over at her, more serious. "We probably do have to hire an exterminator, though. A pro. Bonded."

"What?" Charlene's pulse took off. "Why?"

"I heard sounds in the wall between our bedroom and bathroom last night. Boone's right. We probably have mice or chipmunks. They'll damage the wiring, and they could carry, you know…" he jerked his head sideways, stuck out his tongue and pretending to croak. "…*Monkeypox!*"

Charlene didn't laugh. She looked away. She heard that high-pitched, wounded scream.

He pulled her toward him, softening his voice. "Hey, I know you don't like—"

"It could just be the pipes settling. You know? Old house?"

"Charlene—"

She stood abruptly, frowning. "At least wait out the weekend and see."

"Charlene, we have to—"

"Monday. You can call Monday."

She turned her back on him and walked into the house, letting the screen door slam behind her.

DAY 4

By Saturday morning, Charlene hadn't seen any more mice, alive or dead. She hadn't asked Frank if he'd heard anything else in their bedroom walls, and he hadn't pushed her. She knew he hadn't forgotten, though. Once Frank got his mind working on something, it didn't stop. He was waiting her out, waiting for the right time to bring it up again.

To avoid an ambush, Charlene walked out to the barn and got busy putting it to order. She pulled weeds, moved hay, swept out stalls and spider webs up under the roof. Lunchtime passed. Her stomach grumbled. She worked June. She rode Cash. The old black gelding's hooves plodded slowly, steadily along, 'round and 'round the riding ring, his swishy black tail keeping the flies off them both. Cicadas droned on, their end of summer song rising and falling beneath the hot August sun. She felt herself relax.

"Hey, Chuck," Frank said quietly.

Charlene startled and twisted in her saddle. Frank stood

behind the fence, his cheap, easy-to-sanitize black rubber boots sunk half in the mud. He dug in the pocket of his shorts and pulled out a sugar cube. Cash whinnied and tossed his head away from her, stretching the reins. Charlene tried to pull him back, but Cash would not be governed. He trod over to Frank, snorted, and slurped up the cube.

"Frank, I told you. Not when I'm riding. He's supposed to behave *first.*"

Frank sighed. Cash stepped back and then forward to press his chest against the fence, then lifted his head high. He wanted a neck rub up under his jowls. Frank obliged while Cash munched on his sugar cube. "Oh you big, big guy," he said. "I know I'm your favorite."

"What are you doing out here, Frank?"

He looked up at her, squinting in the bright sun. "I came out to see my favorite human."

She felt a little melty flutter inside.

"And to help out."

Charlene smiled in spite of herself. "Well," she said. "Per usual, everything's done, dude."

"Well, damn," said Frank. "Guess I better head back in." He pretended to be serious, and turned to walk away.

"You *could* water the horses."

"I can?"

"If you wanted to."

"Oh, I want to." He paused and scratched his stubbly chin. "How do I do that?"

She laughed. God, the man was useless! She looked down at him. "There are these things called "buckets" in the barn and a very high tech thingy out in the back field. It's called a water pump."

"Okay."

"Need a diagram? A map?"

He smiled up at her. "No, I think I got it."

He walked toward the barn and Charlene steered Cash toward the stepladder she kept in the corner of the ring. She hopped down and reached under Cash's sweaty belly to unfasten the saddle. He snorted and stamped his feet.

"I know," she said. "You're hot."

As she walked with the saddle into the deep shade of the barn, Frank cried out in the back field, "Ah…shit! Shit!"

Charlene set the saddle down and hurried out. "What's—" Her question died on her lips when she saw the blood and feathers.

Frank had dropped his bucket. At the base of the water pump, beneath the dripping spout, lay what had to be one of Boone's chickens. It was still intact, still surprisingly "real fluffy." Blood was smeared beneath its black, beady eyes. Her empty gut turned sickly.

Frank stuck his booted foot out.

"Oh, Frank, don't."

He kicked it over. The hen's stiff legs pointed straight up, almost comically, at the sky. There was a wound on one of its skinny legs, near the top under the breast. Blood had congealed around it. It was black at the edges. "Weird," he said. "It almost looks like a burn." He stood up and looked around the field, beyond it and into the woods. Charlene stared into the thing's dead black eyes.

"Maybe a fox?" Frank said, his hands on his hips.

"Fox wouldn't have dragged it this far. Probably a coyote."

"You gotta tell Boone."

"Me?" She shook her head vigorously. "Oh no. No, no, no. You do it."

"You're the animal expert."

"But he *likes* you."

Frank grinned a little. "Yes he does. *Fine*. I'll walk over tomorrow." He tapped his index finger on the water pump, thinking. "Are you done here?"

"I have to wipe down Cash and water both horses. Then I'm done."

Frank reached behind his head and dragged off his shirt. He wrapped it around his hand and gingerly picked the chicken up by its leg and threw it into the woods. Back at the house, he torched the shirt.

That night, Frank went back out with her to do the last barn check while the crickets and katydids chirped their hearts out in surround sound. While she worked, Frank shoveled up the bloodied soil under the water pump, deposited it in a trash bag and hosed the area down with a sanitizing solution. "Just in case," he said. Then he walked to the edge of the woods to dispose of the hen.

He shouted to her, "The chicken's gone, Charlene."

"Really?" She stepped out of the barn.

He pulled out a small flashlight and shined it into the dark tangle of bushes and seedlings. "There's a trail of blood heading that way."

The faint scent of charred wood wafted toward her, and she thought she could feel residual heat from the lightning strike. Though the woods were still wet from the rain, and the chance of a fire was remote, she knew she should go check it out. But something kept her rooted in place. Call it intuition. A sixth sense she'd gained from years working around barns, fields and woods. Frank took a step into the wood.

Charlene grabbed his hand.

He looked down at her, worried. "Charlene, I want to buy a gun. If we have coyotes—"

Charlene rounded on him. "Yeah? Will it be a Glock? Or a Wesley & Smith?" The angry sarcasm wasn't lost on Frank.

"Charlene," he said softly.

Charlene's heart pounded like a madman running through her chest. "I'm sorry," she mumbled. She turned to walk away from him.

He followed her back to the barn where she found a crate, tipped it over and sat down. Frank couldn't bring himself to sit on the dirty floor beneath the sticky fly paper, so he stood there, waiting, above her.

Charlene looked down at her hands. "My dad had guns. Rifles. Shotguns. A few semi-automatics. He was a hunter. A collector. He'd grown up in a house with guns, hunting with his father.

Deer. Turkey. Quail." Uneasy, she shifted her weight. "When I was eight he taught me to shoot. We shot cans and bottles at the edge of our property. It was fun." She looked up at him.

"Then he took you hunting."

She curled the fingers of one hand over and dug at the dirt under her nails.

He asked softly, "What was it?"

"A rabbit. I hit it. I didn't kill it." Her heart tripped and stumbled. She could still hear it. She raised her voice to drown it out. "It screamed, Frank. It screamed like a child being tortured." She dropped her hands and looked back up at him. "My dad led me over and told me my rabbit—he said *my* rabbit—was in pain and that I had to take care of that. It was still screaming. It looked so scared."

Cash nickered and swung his head over his stall door to see what was going on. June munched on her hay. Outside, the crickets and katydids went on with their nightly roundup of news or love calls or whatever it was they were trying so hard to say.

"You never told me that," Frank said. "Why didn't you tell me?"

She stared at his knees. "I don't know. I don't. I just…" She felt herself flailing, her brain unwilling to fill in the details.

He crouched down in front of her, his expressive, dark eyes telling her he understood.

Tears pricked her eyes. Her voice caught. "I don't…I don't like to kill things."

"I'd say that's a laudable quality, Chuck." He swept a strand of her hair out of her face. "No guns. Okay. Maybe we could do like...bear spray?"

She snorted a laugh. "Do you have some?"

He smiled. "Not yet."

She was silent a moment, and then she said quietly, "There are mice in the house. I saw mouse poop in our bathroom cabinet two nights ago."

He dropped his head and sighed.

"You really think they're in the walls?"

Frank nodded at the ground. Then he grabbed her hand and hauled her to her feet. "I'm sorry. I heard them again last night. I'll call Monday."

DAY 5

Frank wanted a big, Cheese Bucket-worthy breakfast on Sunday morning. Homemade pancakes as big as dinner plates. Fresh-picked blueberry syrup. Sausage and farm fresh eggs. Instead, they got to work cooking with what they had: Hungry Jack syrup and pancake mix and shaved ham and eggs from Mount Gilead's own Town & Pump Deli.

The eggs were farm fresh.

After the morning barn check, Charlene reminded Frank of his promise to tell Boone about the dead hen. He needed to know so he could protect the chickens he had left. Frank lobbied hard for a neighborly visit on Monday. He said they had unpacking and laundry to do. That he needed to do research on exterminators and bear spray. Research was Frank's rabbit hole. His time-tested method for avoiding things.

"I'll tell you what, François, if you walk over after dinner, I'll come with you."

Frank grinned. "I'll make cookies to take."

By four, the laundry was done, the cookies were made and Frank had disappeared into his bomb shelter to start his research. Charlene tugged on her cowboy boots and called up to him that she was headed out to the barn to work June.

No answer. Probably had his headphones on. Well, she'd never needed a chaperone before, and unless their coyote was rabid, it posed little threat to a full grown human.

She walked to the barn alone.

The wind had picked up, and clouds edged purple and gray had bled into the sky from the west. She was halfway to the barn when she heard the horses' shrill, panicked screaming and hooves kicking stall doors. She broke into a run.

Inside the dark barn, the heavy aroma of horse sweat, smeared manure and thick dust assaulted her nose. Charlene coughed. Cash snorted. June reared and shrieked. With her heart in her throat, she rushed to June's stall.

"Hey, June. Hey…shh." June kicked her door, a hard *thwack* that shook the whole thing on its hinges. The whites of June's eyes flashed as she threw her head. Charlene had to calm her down, and fast, or the mare would break a leg. Cash pawed the floor.

"What's wrong, June? What? *What?*"

The spooked horse backed into the corner of her stall and stared at the wall, her breath steaming in and out of her nose. Had the coyote gotten in here? A bat? Cold flushed under her skin. Was she bitten? Charlene grabbed a flashlight off the tack room shelf and shined it around June's stall. Nothing. Whatever it was, it was gone.

She slowly lifted the latch. "I'm coming in to take a look at you."

June stayed pinned to the back corner of her stall, trembling. Charlene kept her distance. She aimed the light at June's neck, withers and back. A few abrasions, but nothing serious. June snorted and stomped her feet. Charlene moved the beam slowly down her forelegs. More surface scrapes. Charlene breathed easier. She shifted the cone of light to June's hind legs, flashing it over her flank, hocks and—

"Fuck."

A hand-wide, patch of hair and skin was missing from one of her legs a few inches above her hoof. Blood oozed from the open wound.

"Oh, June," Charlene murmured. "What did you do?" She stepped toward her to see the wound better, but slipped on a fresh pile of manure. Charlene went down, the flashlight beam bouncing up into June's face. She quickly tucked and rolled, sure June would react violently to the bright light.

But June didn't move. She didn't blink. She snorted, still shaking, still staring at the damn wall.

Charlene leaned back on her elbows, her ass sunk in warm

horse dung. A stab of fear wobbled in her gut. She looked up at her beautiful horse.

June was blind.

By the time Charlene reached the house to tell Frank and call for help, a black, knotty hole had invaded her chest. Frank hastily searched the internet for a large animal vet available for emergencies and called. The vet said she would be there in an hour.

Charlene wanted to get back to the barn. Was June sick? Infected? Had she hit her head? The two headed out. The damp wind whipped their faces under a grim, overcast sky. Near the barn, Frank stopped and looked toward the woods, toward where he'd tossed the dead chicken. "Do you smell that?"

"Frank—"

"Something's burning."

"Frank, June needs me!"

"Fine. Go. I'll meet you there." He walked into the woods.

Charlene hesitated, knowing she'd been reckless to not check it out days ago. The wind was strong, out of the northwest, and blowing the pungent odor right at them. Charred wood, smoke and something more sinister…decay.

Oh, shit.

"Frank! Wait!" The dark canopy of silver maples and red oaks closed over her as she crashed through the underbrush after him, pushing vines and branches out of her way. She saw him trip and almost go down ahead of her.

"Oh God," he said. "Oh my…ugh. God…"

Charlene caught up to him. He was looking at his feet, horrified. She looked down. His right sandal was tangled up in a possum's ribcage. The thing was mostly bones and slime.

"Oh, God," he said again, gagging. He grabbed her shoulder and tried to shake the bones off his foot.

She knew Frank. The list of possible pathogens was probably expanding rapidly in his head. "You want to go back and... sanitize you ankle?" He didn't answer her. She touched his shoulder. "Frank."

He blinked at her as the last gooey bone slid off. "No." He gagged again. "Sorry...I'm okay."

He bravely pushed on through the ghostly wood to the epicenter of the scorched, mud-spattered trees. Charlene's jaw dropped. Beside her, Frank said, "Holy. Fucking. Shit."

The deep, swampy puddle had dried up revealing a crater at least twelve feet long and two feet deep. Embedded at the far end was a jagged, shiny black rock the size of a basketball. Parts of it had sheared off as it plowed through the earth. The rock itself had cracked open, revealing a smooth hollow center, and steam wafted off it, not smoke. It was the detritus around the rock, on the forest floor, that was smoking.

After four days, the thing was still blistering hot.

She looked back at Frank. He said, "That's a fucking meteorite."

She nodded, dumbfounded, her eyes slowly taking in the rest of the scene. Around the crater, strewn in tangled underbrush, were more dead animals. More bones. Mice. Chipmunks. Another possum and the missing Glock and Smith, or Smith and Wesley. Charlene walked around the crater, inspecting the carcasses. Some were completely stripped of flesh. The few that were still intact had bloody eyes and oozing leg wounds.

"These weren't here five days ago," she said. She bent over near one to get a closer look.

"Get back! Might be contaminated!" Frank cried, then, "Oh man, Charlene, get over here." He covered his nose and pointed. Back in the underbrush, Charlene glimpsed the unmistakable eye-shine of a coyote. "It's dead." He laced his hands over his head. "What could kill a coyote, Chuck?"

The hair stood up on the back of Charlene's neck. There was more going on here than just a coyote kill zone and a dead apex predator. Something felt just…wrong. She closed her eyes and listened.

"Frank," she said slowly. "There's no sound. Listen."

There were no chirping insects. No small, scurrying mammals. No birds. Frank looked back at her, eyes widening. He opened his mouth to respond, but the sound of wheels on gravel punctured the void. A car horn. Leaving the bones behind, they cut swiftly through the woods back to the house.

Panting as they ran, Frank asked again, "What could kill a coyote, Chuck? *Chuck?*"

"I don't know." But she put on a burst of speed, because whatever it was, it posed a threat to full grown humans.

Doctor Jodi Sauer arrived in a Ford Bronco wearing cowboy boots and a floral denim scrunchie around a severe gray ponytail. Her colorless lips were just as severe.

"You say your mare's blind?"

Charlene nodded, breathless from her run. "She just stared at the wall. The flashlight—"

"Lots a reasons a horse might stare at a wall, Mrs. Bouchard. Let's go see." Dr. Jodi grabbed her bag, slammed the truck door shut and strode away from them at a quick pace toward the barn.

Charlene caught a side-eye from Frank. Frank didn't like to be dismissed.

Still shaken by the shiny space rock and bloody boneyard, Charlene's underarms pumped out anxious sweat as the vet asked a slew of basic questions about her horses and their move to the country. A few feet from the barn door, Charlene heard sick, ragged breathing. She reached June's stall and hit her knees. The Buckskin had collapsed with her head resting at an upward, awkward angle against the wall. One of the mare's legs had snapped when she fell, and wet, white bone protruded through. Flies swarmed her eyeballs and wounds.

"Oh God, June, no…no…" Charlene moaned. "No." She reached up to flip off the latch and started to crawl inside. Frank dropped to his knees behind her and wrapped both arms around her waist. He whispered, "We don't know what's wrong with her yet, okay? We don't know. She could be—"

"Oh, for God's sake, Frank! Not everything is about viruses and germs!"

But she let him envelop her with the warmth of his body. Behind them, Cash shuffled in his stall, nervous.

"Lordy," Dr. Jodi said. She glanced in on Cash, then stepped lightly around them into June's stall. "Easy, girl." The young mare flinched, shifting her blind eyes in the vet's direction. The flies lifted. They'd been feeding on shiny wells of blood pooled in the corners of June's eyes. Charlene willed herself not to vomit. The vet performed a cursory exam. She swabbed June's wounds and deposited them in test tubes. She took pictures. There was no point in doing much more. She faced Charlene, her lips set in a practiced, sympathetic line.

"I am so sorry, Mrs. Bouchard. Your horse is indeed blind, and her left foreleg is shattered. The leg will never heal right." She paused to let that sink in. Charlene's breath hiccupped in her chest. "I am truly, *truly* sorry. I can euthanize her now…or you can wait with her while she dies."

Charlene felt Frank's heart beating against her back. She looked at June and leaned into him, hearing the screaming… always the screaming. The horse, *her* horse was in pain. She had to take care of that. She had to—

"Do it. Do it now." Charlene's whole body trembled. Tears streamed down her cheeks. "Please hurry."

Charlene signed papers and the vet quickly administered two injections. After the first, June's head slid slowly down the wall until her nose was on the ground. The mare's eyes closed. After the second, her young muscles jerked, once, twice…then she was gone.

Charlene wiped her eyes. "What happened? Why?"

The vet disposed of the needles and syringes and snapped off her gloves. "I don't know, dear. I'll send the specimens to the lab, but I've never seen anything like it." She leaned back over the horse and pointed to the large wound on June's leg. "See here? That black around the edge? That's necrotizing flesh. And the wound's still oozing blood and lymph hours after it occurred."

Charlene felt weak, but she paid attention. She wanted to know what the fuck had killed her horse. The vet continued on, "And all these little cuts and scrapes? Still bleeding." She stood up and waved at the horse. "Her gums are bleeding. So are her eyes."

"It's hemorrhagic," Frank whispered. He looked up at the doctor. "Rodent poison?"

"No," Charlene stumbled to her feet. "No. I searched the house, the barn, the riding ring the day after we moved in." She wiped her eyes again, swaying. Frank touched her back to steady her. "There were no old packages of poison. No pellets, granules, or discolored soil. No bait boxes. Nothing."

The vet zipped up her bag. "Poison doesn't present like this, Mr. Bouchard. The bleeding, yes, but the blindness, sudden onset, the necrotizing flesh—it's more likely a fast-moving infection."

"Or a snakebite."

Charlene's heart thumped harder as she thought of the bloody kill zone. "Frank, all those animals. Their eyes—"

"I know."

"Slow down." Dr. Jodi leveled a thinly veiled, patronizing gaze at him, and Charlene wondered what the hell the woman's problem was. Her horse had just *died*. "Let's calm down. We got rattlers and copperheads in Ohio, but their venom isn't—"

Frank stabbed a finger at poor bleeding June, and Charlene

winced. "That horse startled at something right before my wife found her," he said. "Gimme the flashlight." She handed it over, and he stepped into the stall and shone the beam around.

The vet chuckled nervously. "You're looking for a viper native to another continent."

"Stupid people buy stupid pets all the time. We had a Bushmaster bite in Cleveland last year." He walked out of the stall. The sun had set and the barn was full of shadows. He swept the light around, morphing them bigger and smaller. "They get tired of them. They let them go. They escape." He turned around to face Charlene and the vet. The light streamed past them. "Boomslangs have hemotoxic venom that can take a man down in three to five days. They bleed to death. Look behind you."

The skin on Charlene's back crawled. She turned.

He pointed with the light. "In the corner."

There was a hole large enough for a groundhog or a skunk to squeeze through with a pile of fresh dirt beside it.

"Mr. Bouchard, snakes don't dig holes."

Charlene pressed her cool, clammy palms against her aching forehead. This was where Frank's "book" knowledge smashed into the real world. She said, "I don't know Boomslangs, honey, but you're more likely to find rattlesnakes and copperheads in the woods, hanging out in dark, enclosed spaces like hollow logs and—"

A bolt of fear thudded in Charlene's stomach. Frank read her face.

"What Charlene?"

"I thought I saw a small snake in our bathroom three nights ago. In the cabinet. I thought I was just seeing things."

He took a deep, quaky breath and nodded. "The noises in the walls."

"And Jesus, I found a dead mouse by the back door. It had oozy blood around its eyes and a wound on its leg."

The vet's switch to full on, unfiltered condescension shocked Charlene. "You're from the city," she said. And there was her problem. The woman thought they were bumbling city folk without a clue. "In the country, one dead mouse hardly—"

"Oh, there's more than one mouse, lady," Frank said. "Follow me." He snatched up another flashlight, shoved it into the small woman's hands and walked out the barn door. Out there, the nearby woods were still a sound vacuum. Night had dropped like a blanket over them. Only the leaves high above rustled in the moaning wind.

Charlene grabbed his arm at the edge of the forest. "If there's a venomous snake out there..." Her voice faltered. She lifted her chin. "I don't want anything else dying tonight. Okay?"

He looked down at her, the crazy in his eyes fading. He pulled her to him. "I'm sorry. I thought…I'm so sorry. I was trying to help."

"It's okay." She pushed him away, biting her lip. Her mind was still working the problem. "A snake wouldn't have dragged all those dead animals back there. The chickens, the possums—those had to be the coyote."

"The coyote's dead, Charlene. Something killed the coyote."

Dr. Jodi aimed her small, inconsequential beam into the inky black. "How many dead animals are we talking about?"

Charlene ignored her. "We did have a barn cat once that died after eating a poisoned chipmunk."

"There you go."

Charlene's head hurt. None of it made sense. A coyote couldn't have killed all those animals in five days, could it? Neither would a snake, unless...unless there was more than one.

The vet asked again. "How many animals dead?"

Frank replied, "Twelve? Fifteen?"

"Sweet Jesus. And they're all bleeding?"

"The ones that still have flesh on them," Charlene said. "The kills are fresh, too. Since Wednesday. We were out there after the meteorite hit."

"Meteorite?"

"It hit during the storm Wednesday night," Frank said. "It's back there, too. Firefighters thought it was a lightning strike." He looked down at Charlene. "We should call NASA up in Cleveland tomorrow. I know a guy."

"Well," Dr. Jodi said. "Well—" She stood there, speechless for a minute, still not a drop of sound emanating from the woods behind her. She rubbed her chin with her whole hand. "Could be a toxin leaking from the meteorite. Or radiation."

"Except," Frank said, "the animals that still had skin on them all had leg wounds."

The vet pursed her lips. She looked from Frank into the dark woods. "I am sorry about your horse, Mr. Bouchard. She was a magnificent animal. It's a true tragedy. I'll drop the specimens off at the lab, and we will get to the bottom of what caused her death. I still believe the idea of an exotic snake roaming your land is farfetched, but these wildlife kills and meteorite?" She shook her head. "That does need looking into. I'll make some calls tomorrow, starting with the health department and sheriff. I'll be back with a team in the morning." She took one last look at the woods and walked back across the field to her truck. She kept the flashlight.

Frank tugged Charlene back into his chest. She resisted, then reached behind him, grabbing fistfuls of his T-shirt, tears welling up in her eyes.

"I'm so sorry," he said. "I'm so sorry." He kissed her forehead. "This is…this is…it's like a nightmare."

Charlene shook her head against his chest, her nose clogged, moaning, "I don't understand."

"Something got her. Something dug its way into the barn and—"

Charlene wrenched herself free. "Cash is still in the barn!"

"Damn it." He took off across the field, sprinting, his flashlight beam bouncing off the weedy grass. He was faster than she was and disappeared into the barn ahead of her. Inside the barn, she found him leaning against Cash's door, elbows propped on top of it, head down, breathing hard. "He's fine. He's okay."

Charlene haltered Cash, clipped on a lead rope, and led him out into the back field. "He'll be safer out here where he can't be cornered." She smacked his rump and set him free. He trotted a few feet, then turned and looked at them, working his mouth, nostrils flared. Old man Cash was confused and afraid.

Frank rubbed his hand through his hair. "What are we going to do Charlene? We can't sleep in the house tonight."

She paced back and forth. She thought of June, poor fucking June, and looked up at Frank. "I'm not leaving Cash."

"Then what? You wanna camp out here with him? The tent's in the house. We can't go back in there. God! This is *insane.*"

Frank was done. She could see it in his eyes. He wanted away from this place with its bleeding dead animals, stalking predators and creepy rocks from space. He liked things predictable. He wanted to be prepared, and tonight, all his preparations had failed him. Fortunately, Frank wasn't the only one who prepared for invaders, microscopic or otherwise, but the idea germinating in her head was dicey. A coyote howled in the distance, spooking Cash, and her mind was made up.

"What time is it?" she asked.

"Why"

"I have an idea."

"*Charlene—*"

"Do you trust me?"

He stared at her. She knew she was a sight. Filthy salt trails streaking down her cheeks, grubby dirt under her fingernails, hay and mud stuck to her jeans, boots and ass. She blew a strand of hair out of her eyes and held her breath. Frank sighed. He looked at his watch.

"It's 10 o'clock."

Charlene hoped it wasn't too late on a Sunday to do what she was about to do, but she had to try. She took Frank's flashlight, grabbed his hand and squeezed. Then she led him around their back field and into the tall grass.

DAY 6
MIDNIGHT

Boone was not from Texas like his absurdly-sized, silver belt buckle implied, but he did know vipers. His father had been a Pentecostal preacher, the snake handling kind, at a tiny church in Appalachia.

"Daddy got bit and died," he said, staring up at their beastly Firethorn. He looked over his shoulder. One of his front teeth was longer than all the others and wobbled as he added, "Snakes gonna do what snakes s'posed to do. That's what I told Mrs. Duschnecki when that python ate her Labradoodly pup. Found it coiled under her bed when she went lookin' for her slippers. Near died of a heart attack. Never knew where it come from. She called me. I'm the neighborhood critter control expert. I got the anticoagulants. The good stuff."

Tonight, Boone hadn't brought "the good stuff." Instead, he had a tightly lidded, ten gallon bucket and what looked like pincer claws on the end of a long metal rod. Night vision goggles were strapped to the top of his head instead of his baseball cap. A pistol that looked old enough to be a Civil War artifact was shoved in the waistband of his pants. Just in case.

"You scared of snakes?" Boone asked. "Want to stay out here?"

Charlene thought of the bloody carnage out in the woods. She thought of June, dead in the barn. She thought of Cash, who would have been next, and curled her hands into viselike fists. She was scared, but rage is more potent. "We're coming."

Frank stood on one foot, quietly fighting with his sandals to get them off. Possum guts tracked across the foyer would be a big "hell no" in his pandemic preparedness manual. "Listen," Frank said. "If one of us gets bit, Snake World up in Crawford County has antivenin."

Boone nodded solemnly. He handed Charlene a lit flashlight that could have doubled for the sun, opened the iron gate and walked through the Firethorn.

The two followed Boone up the porch steps. He peered through the window. The house was dark, and the low hum of electronics and appliances was glaringly absent.

Boone stated the obvious, "Your power's out."

"It's in the walls," Frank said. "Maybe disrupted a wire?"

"Could be. Could be."

They slipped inside where the muffled darkness was unnerving, like the silent woods had been, and listened.

A sharp scraping sound came from upstairs, followed by a click, click…*click*.

"Bingo," Boone whispered. He turned to lean his long face into theirs. His sour breath smelled like onions and red meat. "Let's go."

They crept up the stairs behind him. A stair creaked, and Boone froze. Something upstairs scraped again and…click, click, *click*.

The noise came from their bedroom. Charlene aimed Boone's flashlight up past his saggy ass. Boone reached the landing and angled his own light down the hall through their bedroom door, which stood ajar. The hall seemed to lengthen. The dark room beyond it swelled with malignance. Boone poked the bedroom door open, carefully, with his metal pole's pincers.

Scrape. Click, click…*click.*

There was something there. Something heard them. Something knew they were coming for it. Did a snake click? She didn't think so. She didn't know how it could. Her blood chilled.

"Frank, I—"

"Time to switch off that light, Mrs. Bouchard," Boone whispered.

Charlene had the strong urge to grab Frank's hand and tear back down the stairs. He grabbed hers instead. "It's okay. We'll stay way back." His palms were sweating and there was an excited edge to his voice.

Charlene switched off her flashlight. Boone turned off his own and dragged down his goggles. The little red lights around the edges glowed in the dark. In the bedroom, the smell of the musty farmhouse closed in around her. Boone motioned toward their bathroom. "Where's the door?"

Scrape…*click.*

The pocket door was hidden inside the wall. Every muscle in Charlene's body pulled tight. She pointed at the wall and then at the latch. Frank touched the back of her T shirt, the tips of his fingers digging into her skin as he grabbed hold.

Boone grasped the butt of his pistol with a knobby hand, and hooked the tip of a pincer through the latch with the other. Then he pulled.

The massive door rumbled as it ground against the floor.

At first, Charlene couldn't see much, but as the door slid slowly open, her eyes adjusted to the dark, and she saw the shadowy outline of a fleshy, flat snake stretching diagonally across it. The snake was narrower near the door's lower right corner and bulged wider up near the middle, and she wondered, with a cold shiver, what its last meal had been. The door kept sliding and grinding, and the snake held its position on the recessed wood panel like it was glued in place. Charlene had seen her share of snakes, and this one was all wrong. She backed into Frank and glanced up. Another giant, fleshy snake lay flush against the panel, this one stretching diagonally up toward the door's upper right corner.

"Christ on a biscuit," Boone whispered, awed. "There's two of 'em."

Boone kept pulling. The two snakes kept widening, widening, until they joined together in a glistening, pale mound. There were dark striations running across its middle. Warty protrusions and small, dark, spherical bubbles. Frank dragged Charlene back, the neck of her T-shirt pulling tight across her throat. "That's not a Boomslang! That's not a—"

The tip of the snake near the door's upper right corner started to move.

Scrape...*click*.

"Shoot! Oh...*shoot!*" Boone gasped, fumbling his pistol out of his pants.

Scrape...click, *click.*

The grotesque creature drew its arms inward, dragging its claws across the door, leaving deep grooves in the wood, and curled them around the wall's edge.

"Oh fuck!' Frank shouted, backing farther into the room. "Fuck!"

Charlene groped madly at her flashlight, trying to switch it back on.

The thing pulled the rest of its body out from inside the wall, revealing two more fleshy arms. The dark striation across its middle swelled. Boone's hands shook so hard he dropped his gun. He turned to run. The striation split open wide, revealing long, dripping fangs ringing a huge hole. A mouth. A monster's mouth. Boone reached the bedroom door. Two of the monster's arms coiled and snapped toward the terrified man, thinning as they lengthened to at least ten feet. They punctured Boone's waist, hoisting him off his feet, and sprang back. The man screamed.

Frank pushed Charlene toward the bedroom door.

"Go! Go!"

The thing's bulbous middle puffed up like a bloated jellyfish. It rolled onto its back and punctured Boone with its other two terrifying, starfish-like arms. Black bubbles on its skin popped. A banana-like scent filled the room. Oh, the poor man.

"CHUCK! NOW!"

Charlene edged right, her feet threatening to slip out from

under her. Frank pushed her hard. She picked up speed. As she darted through the door, she saw Boone's head disappear into the thing's mouth.

Charlene turned to run down the stairs. A crash rang out from their bedroom and a long, stretchy tentacle whipped out of the bedroom and wrapped around the bannister, barring her way. Its claws hit the wood.

Click...*click.*

Every hair on her body stood on end. Charlene pivoted and raced down the hall toward the bomb shelter. Frank cried out in pain. She heard him stumble behind her. She turned to help, but he'd already regained his footing. *"Go! Go!"* With Frank at her heels, she dove into the room, slamming the door behind them. Frank locked it.

Scrape. Click...*click.*

The doorknob shivered.

SMACK! SMACK!

Two of the things arms hit the wood near the top.

Charlene backed away from it toward the room's window.

Scrape. *SMACK! SMACK!*

The two arms hit again, harder, this time driving long, black iron claws through the solid oak door. The two claws cut downward, making long, jagged rifts in the wood.

Frank glanced at his desk, which was to the left of the door, at his new flip phone lying on a stack of papers. The doorknob rattled. He reached for it.

SMACK! SMACK!

The creature's two other arms hit the door, pounding two more long claws through it. Charlene wrapped her fingers around Frank's waistband and yanked him backward. He cussed, spun and pushed her toward the window. As they passed his shelves, he grabbed a clear plastic bin and shoved it into her hands. Frank was sweating, his lips clamped tight together as he strained to open the window. The door behind them splintered all the way down the middle.

"Knife! Gimme that knife!" he shouted, pointing at the top shelf.

Charlene grabbed the oversized pocket knife and tossed it. He flicked it open and slit the paint gluing the window shut and shoved the knife in his back pocket. He gripped the window again, slamming it upward, and kicked out the screen with his bare foot. Charlene swung a leg over the sill and clambered out. Frank climbed out after her and slammed the window shut, and they slid down the gritty shingles toward the gutter.

Frank grabbed the bin from her and tossed it over the edge into the bushes. He slid over the gutter carefully, hooking his feet on the porch railing below and reached a hand up to her. The window smashed behind Charlene. Flying glass hit the back of her neck. Something cold and fleshy prodded her between her shoulder blades. She jumped, clutching Boone's flashlight against her chest, tucking and rolling like she did when she was thrown from a horse. She hit the ground hard. Her teeth clacked together. She bit her tongue. She saw stars, and her mouth filled with salty blood. Frank dragged her to her feet, cussing a string of obscenities as he limped with her through the gate and slammed it behind them.

They went for the Subaru first. The doors were locked.

Charlene looked around wildly. She had no idea how fast the monster was, but she was certain she couldn't outrun it. "The truck!" she gasped. "Boone's truck!"

They stumbled across the gravel to the rusty truck. The driver's side door was locked. They clawed their way around to the other side. The passenger door swung open. Frank tossed the plastic tub into the back seat, shoved her in ahead of him, crawled in behind her and yanked the door shut. He was sweating profusely. Charlene swallowed the blood in her mouth. Nausea overwhelmed her, and she shook her head fiercely to get a grip.

"Do you see it?" Frank hunched down low in the old truck's passenger seat, head below the window. His seat was ripped and spotted with mold. He gritted his teeth to stifle a groan. "Is it coming?"

"Are you okay?" Charlene searched him frantically with her eyes. One leg of his jeans was ripped above his muddy bare foot. There was blood. "Did it get you?"

"Goddamn it, Charlene! Is it coming?"

Crouching low on the driver's side, Charlene peeked out the driver's side window at the farmhouse. The front door gaped under the new moon. The door quivered in the night breeze, but the foyer and front hall were empty. Her heart beat a warning drum in her ears.

"No. I don't think—"

Gravel crunched and slid on the other side of the passenger door. Terror blazed down Charlene's spine. She mouthed, "It's on your side."

Frank started to inch up to see. She grabbed his sweaty hand and pulled him down. "Don't."

He yanked his hand free and inched up higher, but stopped suddenly, buried his hands in his hair and turned toward her, eyes wide, terrified.

"Chuck…I can't see."

Sour dread slid down her throat. She swallowed and grabbed his hands in both of hers.

His voice trembled and cracked. "Nothing…it's all black."

"Okay," Charlene whispered. "Okay." She drew his cold fingers to her lips and breathed on them softly. "I'm here. I've got you." She felt his pulse with her fingertips. Fast, but steady, considering. Tears rose in Frank's eyes. Not bloody. Not yet.

"My leg," he said through clenched teeth. "It stings like a mother—"

Something bumped and scraped against his side of the truck, rocking the car off its passenger side tires. Frank snatched his hands back. The car bounced down. Charlene sat up and ran her hands frantically over the dashboard, over the visor, around the driver's seat, searching for the truck's keys.

Frank sucked in his breath. "Did you find them?"

"Not yet."

The monster's claws scratched over the rear bumper.

Her eyes flashed to the rearview mirror. She saw the tip of

one of its wrinkled arms slide back off the lift gate. She reached over Frank and punched open the glove box, rifling through the contents. There were coupons for the Grill & Chill and Golden Corral, faded car registrations and folded county maps so old they nearly broke apart in her fingers. She crouched to look under the driver's seat. No keys, but there was a large white, cellophane-wrapped package. She tugged it out.

Tannerite. The word was stamped on a bright orange label over a bullseye. If the explosive targets were in the truck, maybe the gun was, too.

She squeezed between the front seats and tumbled into the back. Shoving Frank's plastic tub aside, she felt around in the dark, finding jackets and a blanket smelling of body odor. She plunged her fingers into a waxy, half empty cup in the drink holder. From the smell, curdled coffee. She turned her attention to the floor. Her fingertips rammed into a hard vinyl case. *Bingo.*

Frank's voice edged higher. "Maybe we could try to hotwire it? Huh?"

"Maybe?"

She unlatched the case. It was dark, and she couldn't be sure, but she thought it contained the pieces of an AR 15. From the shape of the logo, a LaRue. Charlene searched the case. No ammo, but she found a velvet pouch with a small key. She popped up to look out the back window and swept her eyes over the truck bed and then straight down. There. A steel locker was bolted behind the cab below the window. It was padlocked shut. She'd bet her life he stored his ammo in that locker, but with that thing out there—

Frank let out a piercing scream. Charlene stowed the key in her hip pocket and slid back between the seats. He was clutching his leg below the knee so tight his knuckles were white. "Fuck, it burns."

She gently pried his fingers loose. "Let's take a look."

He cried out as she parted the torn flaps of his jeans, rocking in his seat. Her head reeled at the sight of the wound. Like June's, all of his skin in a four inch wide swath had been stripped from around his leg between the ankle and calf. It oozed clear, blood-tinged fluid. Blisters had formed around the edge, and near the back, in the center of his Achilles, was a deep puncture wound. The liquid pooled in the small hole was bright red. Charlene covered her mouth, tears welling up, glad he couldn't see it. "It's not so bad."

"You don't sound so sure, Chuck."

"Your foot's still attached, so..."

"So, *necrosis*. You'll have the pleasure of watching it turn black and drop off." He gestured blindly over his shoulder. "Get the tub."

Something rammed against the truck's underbelly, launching it a few inches off all four tires. Charlene's teeth smacked together again when it crashed back to earth, missing her tongue this time. Frank gripped his moldy seat like he was afraid it might eject him. The monster scratched and clicked across the muffler, the fuel line, the wheels. They heard a loud pop and a soft hiss, and the forward corner of the truck, driver's side, began to sink. Three more pops in quick succession and the whole truck eased down.

Operation Hotwire crashed and burned.

Frank balled his right hand into a fist and pounded it against the door. "God! Get the fucking tub! Please!"

Breathing fast, her fingers trembling, Charlene tore off the lid.

He said, "What's in it?"

"Bandages. Pills. Shots. Scissors."

He rubbed his sweaty forehead with the back of his hand. His whole body was trembling now. "Which shots?"

Charlene picked up the vials, squinting in the dark. "Vitamin K."

"Hopefully, that's a point for us. Gimme one. Fuck it. Gimme two."

"Jesus, Frank, what were these for?"

He laughed. "Ebola. It was a kit. The antivirals were stashed in the little fridge, but I don't need those because I don't have Ebola. I was bitten by a goddamned alien starfish that slimed out of a fucking meteorite, ate its way to the top of the food chain and…" He rambled on, his words slurring a bit, like he might be going delirious.

Charlene cut him off with a shrill, "What do they do, Frank?"

"It's for the bleeding, Charlene! Am I bleeding yet?"

She snapped to attention, her eyes focusing on his. The whites of his eyes were lacy red, the rims were bright red and a bubble of thin liquid clung to the tip of his nose.

Blood.

She snatched up a syringe. They were already loaded.

"Charlene?"

She removed the cap, held it up, squeezed out some of the serum like she'd seen vets do, and pulled his left arm toward her. "You're going to feel a pinch."

Frank brushed his thumb across the tip of his nose and rubbed the slippery liquid between his thumb and forefinger. He sagged in his seat, leaning his head back. He didn't flinch when she sank the first shot. As she readied the second, he dropped his chin and whispered, "How long do you think I have?"

She thought about June's death. The mouse she'd found by the back step. Boone's chickens.

Her voice trembled. "Help's coming. Vet said she'd bring a team in the morning."

She pushed the second plunger and withdrew the needle.

Frank winced, his fists and the color of his face going white. Either from pain or the poison, he was going into shock. She pawed through the box, reading labels on pill bottles. Antibiotics. Paracetamol. Oxycodone. She popped off the Oxycodone cap, tipped two tablets onto her palm and held them to his lips.

"Open."

He pushed her hand away. "Charlene…how long?"

"An hour, maybe two," she said. Tears rolled down her cheeks. "Oh God…I'm sorry…I'm so—"

He felt for her hands, his movements clumsy, and wrapped his fingers around them. Tight. So tight she was sure his fingers would sink into her skin. "It's not your fault. Hey, it's not your fault."

Charlene was openly sobbing now.

"Chuck…Chuck, I love you." He gritted his teeth. "And you're going to *survive*, because when I die tonight—"

"No…no…"

"*Listen* to me. When I'm gone, you open this door and let that fucking monster have me…"

"Oh God…"

"…and then you sprint to the back field and ride your ass out of here. Cash is old, but he's still fast, and…"

"Frank, please stop—"

"…and you *live*, because you have to. I have to know you're going to make it. *Please*." Charlene stared into Frank's sightless eyes. His tears overflowed, and they were red, blood red. "Now give me the pills. Gimme…ten."

She heard her rabbit screaming. She heard her horse screaming. She heard her husband, her best friend, pleading. Her responsibility. They were her responsibility. She bobbed her chin up and down, but before she could speak, behind Frank's head, one of the monster's arms snaked up over the glass. Then another. Then the whole creature slimed over the window. Black bubbles popped around its mouth hole, which opened, huge and round, steaming up the glass, and that sweet, overripe odor she'd smelled up in their bedroom filled the cab.

The thing had stung him.

The thing wanted him.

It was waiting.

Something wild rose up inside her. Something steel hard,

fierce and free. She screamed, "Over my dead fucking body!"

Frank barely flinched. His eyelids slid half closed. "Charlene?"

She grabbed Boone's flashlight, switching it on. She wanted to see this thing in all its hideous, horrifying, alien glory. She swung it around, aiming the blinding beam into its gaping mouth.

The thing shrieked and leaped off the window, crashing across the gravel into the tall grass beyond. Charlene froze, her heartbeat tick, tick, ticking in her ears. Images flooded her mind.

The explosive, slippery movement inside the bathroom cabinet.

The shiver of the shadowy prairie grass.

The dark stable.

The dark hole.

She grabbed Frank's face with both hands. "I'm not letting you go, François." She kissed him softly on the lips, then shoved the two pills between them.

"Chuck?"

She climbed into the backseat with Boone's flashlight. She opened the case. It was a LaRue. Charlene knew guns. Her dad had taught her everything he knew, and his LaRue had been his prized possession. It was one of the most consistently accurate AR 15's out there.

"Chuck!"

"It's okay, honey. I got a plan." She snapped the gun together. It smelled like cold steel, smoke and retribution.

She sighted the rifle through the window and swung the barrel to the left, searching, then to the right. Nothing.

It was out there.

It was only a matter of time before it smashed the windows of the broken down truck, and there was no way in hell she was feeding Frank to an alien. She slid her hand behind Frank's back. He winced. "Sorry." She dug the knife out of his back pocket and used it to slit the cellophane wrapper on the Tannerite.

There were three canisters and instructions. She skimmed them faster than she should have, but the concept was simple. There were two kinds of granules. Separate—it was harmless. Mixed and pierced by a large caliber bullet speeding two thousand feet per second—

BOOM!

She wiped her sweaty forehead and then dumped the contents of the two Tannerite canisters together in the mixing jar. She screwed it shut and shook it up and down while a voice inside her head scolded her for her lack of care with explosives. She shook the jar harder, and then she looked at Frank. Her husband looked so sick, and that electrified her.

She quickly dragged her shirt off over her head and carefully, gently, wiped the blood from his eyes and nose and then wrapped the mixed Tannerite up in her bloody shirt.

"Frank, my love," she whispered. "I'm going to go blow some shit up."

With sweat and blood gleaming on his face, he smiled weakly. "You never promised me quiet…Chuck." Charlene kissed his forehead.

Then she kicked her cowboy boot through the rear window,

smashing it to pieces.

Charlene used the barrel of the gun to poke out the stubborn glass still clinging to the edges of the window frame. Kneeling on the backseat, she stuck the flashlight out and swept it across the tall grass behind the truck, over the gravel drive to her left and the Firethorn to her right. She sat back on her heels, twisted around and flashed the powerful beam through the front windshield, listening to Frank breathe.

She sank her fingers into the bloody shirt, wrapping them around the Tannerite, and crawled partway out the rear window. When her shoulders were clear, she cocked her hand back and threw the bloody ball as hard as she could. She heard it hit the gravel behind the truck, a little to the left, and ducked back inside.

She turned off the flashlight and listened.

The west wind played with her long, messy braid and whispered across her sweaty skin. Her heart pounded like a whole field of Thoroughbreds. The gravel surrounding the truck was like a thousand trip wires. If the creature came within thirty feet of her, she'd know. She listened.

Precious seconds ticked by.

Nothing moved.

Nothing *moved.*

She pressed her palms against her forehead. Maybe she was wrong. Maybe the thing didn't have a taste for him. Maybe it wouldn't go for only a morsel. Damn it. *Damn it.* The LaRue was a powerful weapon, but she'd watched enough alien movies with Frank to suspect that, without the Tannerite in that thing's belly, the bullets would just piss it off. She couldn't wait any longer. She had to get the ammo, hunt it down and hope for the best.

She turned the flashlight back on and stuck it back out the rear window, hoping the light would deter the thing long enough for her to get the bullets. With the gun looped over her shoulder and the key in her hand, she eased out and crouched down quickly in front of the locker, balancing the light on her knees. She fit the key in the lock. When the lock sprang open, she nearly cried.

The truck swayed under her feet. Could've been the wind, but she wasn't counting on it. She threw open the locker and raked her fingers through it, grabbing the first thing they touched and stood up, spinning to swing the beam a full 360 degrees. All quiet, but her skin prickled. Something was wrong. Something was…missing. She cut the flashlight beam back to flood the area behind the truck with light. There was a smear of blood on the gravel. No balled up shirt. The shirt was gone.

The pounding of her heart stopped.

She glanced down at the object in her hand. A weighted down black pillowcase. The ammo. She plunged her hand inside, but the whole truck suddenly pushed up, up, up under her boots and tilted over. She toppled out. The pillowcase and flashlight flew out of her hands, and the truck kept rolling. She squeezed her eyes shut as it tumbled over her onto its back.

Charlene groaned, stunned and disoriented. Her back and head ached. Her ears rang. She turned her face, pressing her cheek into sharp gravel. A dozen yards away, the flashlight stood on end in front of the Firethorn, shooting its beam straight up into the sky like a life flight beacon. Beyond it lay the pillowcase.

Gravel scraped and slid near her feet. Charlene twisted onto her stomach, pushed up onto her elbows and army-crawled out from under the truck. Her back screamed. Her head throbbed. Claws raked the other side of the lift gate.

Scrape, *click!*

She pushed up onto her feet.

Scrape, click...*click!*

She sprinted the last few yards and bent to snatch up the flashlight. Something wrapped around her boot and yanked her legs out from under her. She reached for the light with the tips of her fingers as she went down, missing. Her chin scraped through the gravel as the monster dragged her backward.

"No!" she cried. She saw Frank's dark expressive eyes. His bloody, dying eyes. Her gut clenched. "No!" She spat blood from her mouth and kicked backward, desperately wiggling her ankle and foot inside her trapped boot. Her foot popped free. She lunged forward, grabbed the flashlight and swung it around, hitting the alien dead center in its hungry, drooling mouth. The monster let out an otherworldly screech, slowing, but its momentum carried it forward. On her back, Charlene threw her hands up to shield her face. The thing's slick, fleshy appendages spiraled forward, their clawed tips missing her forearms by inches. Then the monster turned and ran smack into the Firethorn.

The motherfucker was caught, spread eagle, on the wicked bush. Every time it moved, the finger-long thorns tore through its thin skin. Smelly, blue blood splashed bright orange berries.

Charlene held her nose as she reached for the pillowcase. She pulled out a magazine, slammed it into the gun and stumbled to her feet.

A sound like a dying space whale beached on an asteroid belt bled from the creature's quivering mouth. She shined the flashlight down it one more time just to hear it scream. Then she backed up all the way up to the truck, braced the stock of the gun against her shoulder, hearing her dad's voice. *You have to take care of that.*

She pulled the trigger.

The explosion slammed her body back into the cab. Thorns peppered her skin. Pieces of flaming alien flew over the truck, over the farmhouse and into the wildflowers. The Firethorn caught fire. Picking pieces of drippy tentacle off her chest and chin, she limped to the other side of the tipped over truck to check on Frank.

Frank, her pandemic-planning nut, had belted himself in. His head lolled, but he was in one piece. Blood dripped from his nose onto the cab ceiling

"Frank? Can you hear me? Frank! *Frank!*"

He was unconscious, but still breathing. She crawled in through the window and slid beneath him, unbuckling his seatbelt and using her body to ease him down. She dragged him out of the car, then crawled back in to search through the mess inside. She needed the county maps, one map in particular. When she found it, she sprinted through her blazing Firethorn into the house.

DAY 21

Crack! Crack!

Charlene fired over her dying wildflowers at the target a hundred feet away. A breeze with a bite to it rippled through the field. The leaves of the oaks and maples in her wood were turning orange, red and brown above a small army of humans in dark suits combing the cool ground beneath them. Glorious autumn and the Men in Black had arrived in Mount Gilead. Charlene wondered how long they'd stay.

She fired again.

Crack!

She was sore. The LaRue, which she had unapologetically commandeered as her own, had bruised her shoulder.

"Missed again."

Charlene turned around, hand on hip. Frank sat in a camp chair with his wind up radio squawking on his lap and retro sunglasses hiding his eyes. He said, "Even a blind man could tell that you suck, Chuck." The wind stirred his hair.

"I have lots of bullets, François."

"Sounds like you're gonna need 'em."

She turned back around, sighted the rifle, sucked in her breath and let it out slow. She pulled the trigger.

BOOM!

Frank clapped his hands. She walked over, grabbed his water bottle out of his drink holder and drained it. The blue merle puppy hopping around his only foot barked up at her. She crouched down to scratch behind the dog's ears. "I'll get him another one, Boone." The little Aussie pup was already protective of Frank. Charlene kissed Frank on the lips, and he pulled her down onto his lap, while the man on the radio read the news.

"Hello, Mansfield. It's Saturday, August 16, 2003. The Morrow County Health Department claims the man who was treated for a rare case of hemorrhagic fever at Morrow County Hospital has been released and is recovering well at an undisclosed location. Hospital officials have insisted the infection was the result of a lab accident, and the virus involved is not easily transmissible and has been contained. The investigation is ongoing."

"You're so famous," Charlene teased.

"At least I'm not wanted by the law," Frank teased back, and as the newsman kept talking he waved at the radio. "Yeah! See?"

"In other news, there are still no suspects for the break-in two weeks ago at Snake World in rural Crawford County. In a press conference this morning, the sheriff confirmed that the cameras in the building were blown out by an AR 15 rifle, possibly a LaRue, and that the only item missing was the entertainment venue's entire supply of Boomslang snake antivenin. The owner has assured the sheriff's office that all of his resident Boomslang snakes are accounted for."

Frank leaned in to whisper in her ear, "Did you have a lot of bullets when you shot out those cameras? Because...you would have needed a lot of bullets."

She slapped his arms away, stood up and walked toward the woods. "Tell your dog to get your water. I have to see what the alien wranglers are up to." The newsman's voice faded behind her.

"It's going to be another cold, clear evening here in Mansfield. Make sure to step outside around midnight and look up. A meteor shower is headed our way and they say it will be spectacular."

THE END

DUBLIN CREATIVE WRITERS COOPERATIVE

The Dublin Creative Writers Cooperative is a group of working writers in the Columbus, Ohio area. We aim to provide a supportive and constructive environment for fiction writers of all genres and experience levels. Our meetings include write-ins, technical/craft workshops, writing contests, social events, and group critique sessions.

To join, visit our Meetup page.

Receive practical, transformative writing & publishing tips!
Subscribe to our blog:

HTTPS://WWW.DUBLINCREATIVEWRITERS.COM/BLOG

DESIDERIUM: An Anthology

Presented by Dublin Creative Writers Cooperative

JULY 2021

AUTHOR BIOS

A. Howitt loves dogs, jelly beans, slipper socks, and board games. A writer since 2001, she developed a taste for reading when she found the Laura Ingalls Wilder books, and quickly fell in love with history and fantasy stories from her dad's collection. Her hobbies include sewing, gardening, sword-fighting, costuming, archery, dancing, and being outdoors. As a lifelong artist, she's been competing in art contests off and on for more than a decade, and has LEGO displays shown in the Columbus Museum of Art.

J. Levesque writes poetry, suspense, thrillers, and unreliable memoirs. She has been published in *Oasis*, and her poetry chapbooks *Haiku* and *Simmer*, are available on Amazon, as are her science fantasy novels *Dominion of the Lost* and *Dominion of the Hidden*, which are written under the pen name, Jora Dublinn. Her work can be found at **jlevesque.website** and **joradublinn.com**.

Thomas Brown woke one morning, certain he was dead. But he was just in the Mid-West. He tries to live and write pulp there. Find him at **tbrownlbtf@gmail.com**.

Anne Johnston is the pen name of a recent escapee from the strictly non-fiction world of academia now writing contemporary and speculative fiction. Her debut anthology of short stories,

Wish Upon a Pocketwatch, is available on Amazon, and she is currently working on the first book of her Lamplight Series.

Anne works in the thrilling world of state government and statistics and lives in Ohio with her husband and mother. When not at her day job or busy writing, Anne spends time contemplating the tricky nature of life and wishes from her kayak. Find her on Instagram **@annejohnstonwrites**. Website: **https://annejohnstonwrites.wixsite.com/author**

Autumn Shah writes fiction and creative nonfiction. She lives in the suburbs of Columbus, Ohio. Her creative nonfiction has been published in several literary journals and you can read some of her writing at: **https://myshamelesswonder.blogspot.com/**.

J. H. Schiller is a science fiction and fantasy author who lives and writes in Ohio. She is currently querying her first novel, *Buttermilk Sky*, a contemporary fantasy, and working on *The Witch of Tophet County*, a contemporary fantasy of equal parts humor and drama. She can be found at **jhschiller.com**.

Tom MacMahon is a bilingual native of Canada who has lived in the US for the last twenty years. He is an emerging writer whose interest lies in the more esoteric content such as ghost stories and the occult. Tom holds degrees in Communications, Physics & Chemistry and Education. Tom runs a small event business out of Columbus.

George Mason, originally from the Washington, D.C., area, is a retired law enforcement and intelligence officer who now resides in Ohio and Florida. An author of numerous professional articles and texts, he is currently working on his first novel, expected in the Fall of 2020.

J. Powell Ogden lives in Dublin, Ohio and graduated from The Ohio State University. She writes horror, science fiction, techno-thriller and young adult dark fantasy. She is also the CEO and creative director of Spark Street Media, LLC, a small press publishing company. Find out more: **jpowellogden.com** & **sparkstreetmedia.com**.